AMBUSH!

Four dark figures rose suddenly from behind a thick clump of brush and a spinning lariat tightened around Marshall's arms, jerking him out of the saddle.

The outlaws jumped him as he struggled desperately to free himself. He drew up his right leg and drove it viciously into one bandit's face. He butted another with his head and rolled away from a third.

He was on his knees still fighting when a gun butt crashed against his head, ending his bid for freedom.

"There he is—sleepin' beauty," one of the killers laughed. He aimed his gun. "I'm gonna save the town the price of a hangin'."

GUNSMOKE IN PARADISE

Burt Arthur

BELMONT TOWER BOOKS • NEW YORK CITY

A BELMONT TOWER BOOK

Published by

Tower Publications, Inc.
Two Park Avenue
New York, N.Y. 10016

GUNSMOKE IN PARADISE

CHAPTER 1

IT WAS LATE afternoon of an early September day and the air was surprisingly cool and crisp. Evidently summer was finally drawing to a close—a summer that had seemed unending, with long wearying days, one hard upon the other almost without respite, each oppressively hot, overpowering and toll-taking. Now a stiff, chilling breeze droned over the prairie land, humming a whispered warning that the night would be a cold one. It whined through the thinning brush, whirled about aimlessly for a moment, gathering momentum, then swerved and raced southward toward the sheltered valleys. Dust and vagrant leaves, sun-dried, brown and crisped to the point of crumbling, were caught up by the wind and swirled about in short-lived flight.

Presently, a lone horseman astride a big black horse halted on the horizon, an eerie, spectral figure silhouetted against the sky. The man relaxed in his saddle for a minute, shifted himself and looked about him. Far to the north he could see a broken range of hump-backed hills, desolate and barren, brooding in sullen silence.

To the east and to the south, as far as the eye could see, the range spread away in green-brown, billowing waves of thin, short-cropped grass. The uneven ground gave the appearance of a wrinkled, two-toned carpet of inestimable length and breadth.

To the west, that vast untrod and unsullied expanse of promised land, there was a fast-fading glow in the sky—the reflection of the setting sun.

The wind rose again, and Marshall snapped up the collar of his leather jacket, buttoning it snugly around his neck. The black snorted and pawed the hard ground impatiently.

7

"Go 'head," Marshall said curtly, blowing on his hands. He settled himself in the saddle.

The big horse jogged off.

"Well?" his rider demanded tauntingly. "Thought yuh wanted to get goin'? Fr'm th' way yuh're amblin' along, I reckon you ain't in such a hurry after all. It's awright with me, y'know, if we gotta camp out here f'r th' night—I got a warm blanket. But what yuh're gonna do t' keep fr'm freezin' —we-ll, you better figger that out f'r y'self."

The black bounded away. His flashing hoofs pounded and echoed over the cold ground. Marshall pulled the brim of his hat down over his eyes, buried his chin in his upturned collar and settled himself a bit more comfortably in the saddle. Then with startling suddenness the big horse jerked to a stiff-legged halt, almost jolting his rider out of the saddle.

"What in blazes—" Marshall yelled. He straightened up in the saddle, stemming the torrent of words that came to his lips, looked hard and muttered a simple but significant, "Oh."

Just ahead of them lay the sprawled-out figure of a man, face downward in the dirt and grass. The man's left arm was outstretched toward a rifle that lay but inches beyond his reach. His right arm was doubled up under him. Marshall frowned. He studied the prone figure for a moment.

"Hey!"

There was no response, no movement from the man, not even the barest twitching of a muscle to indicate that he was alive, and that he had heard Marshall's voice. The latter dismounted stiffly, stamped his booted feet on the ground, loosened one of his Colts in its holster and trudged forward. He came up slowly behind the man, looked down at him, circled him warily, kicked the rifle out of the way, halted finally and bent over him and turned him over on his back. One look was sufficient. The man was dead. There was a single, black-rimmed bullet hole midway between his sightless eyes.

"Dead, awright," Marshall muttered. "Dead's he'll ever be. Bullet got 'im plumb center."

He studied the dead man's face for a minute. It was the face of a middle-aged man, deeply lined, sun-bronzed and wind-toughened, and now it was rigid in death. Marshall shook his head. He straightened up slowly.

8

"Leave it t' me," he mumbled disgustedly, "t' stumble over somethin' like this. Never seen it t' fail."

He turned slowly, his keen eyes probing the ground around the outstretched body. He turned his back to the wind and the swirling dust. When they subsided again, he cursed angrily, for the wind had whipped the dust about in such fashion that it had completely obliterated whatever footprints or other identifying clues the killer might have left behind him. Then something caught his eye—a piece of paper impaled upon a sharp-tipped branch in amidst a clump of brush. Marshall sauntered over and removed the paper and looked it over idly. It had been folded in two originally; the dividing line was still there. It was soiled and finger-marked, proof that it had received a good deal of handling. There was a red seal in one corner, identifying it as a legal document. Marshall scanned it. It was a deed to a ranch and it had been issued in the name of one Jim Halliday.

"Registered in Paradise," Marshall muttered. "Never heard o' that town b'fore. 'Course that don't prove that there ain't such a place—specially after bein' in towns named Hell an' Heaven."

He considered returning the deed to the dead man's shirt pocket, but decided against it and pocketed it himself instead, retraced his steps and halted again beside the outstretched body and looked down at it.

"Reckon I'll hafta do somethin' 'bout you, Mister," Marshall said presently, half aloud. "Can't take yuh with me an' I can't leave yuh layin' there like y'are. Th' wolves an' th' coyotes'd make short work of yuh."

He strode over to his horse, unstrapped his new blanket, eyed it and shook his head sadly, opened it and spread it over the dead man and weighted it down with heavy rocks. After a few minutes he stepped back and surveyed his work, then, apparently satisfied that the body would be safe and unmolested, at least until he could reach the nearest town and notify the sheriff and have that worthy come for it, nodded to himself, wheeled and returned to the waiting black. He caught up the reins and swung himself into the saddle. He nudged the big horse with his knees. The black snorted, backed a bit, swung wide around the blanketed body and cantered away.

It was dusk now and dark, and the rugged hills to the north

were fading away into shadowy nothingness. As they whirled past a thick clump of brush, a dark figure suddenly arose and a lariat shot out, looping in a swiftly widening circle over the head of the unsuspecting and momentarily unwary Marshall. Instinctively but too late the big black checked himself and tried frantically to swing wide to avoid the snaking rope. The spinning lariat settled around Marshall's arms, tightened like a flash and jerked him out of the saddle. He struck the hard ground with a stunning crash.

Shadowy figures arose now and bounded out from behind the brush. One man lunged for the black's bridle but the big horse screamed, reared and lashed out with lightening hoofs, and the man backed away hastily. The black retreated too, snorting loudly. Other men pounced upon Marshall and pinned him down.

He struggled desperately to free himself, drew up his right leg and drove it viciously into a man's face. He heard the man cry out and knew that his spurred bootheel had lessened the odds against him. He butted another man with his head, rolled away from a third attacker and had fought his way to his knees when a gun butt, thudding against his head, ended his brief bid for freedom. He grunted, and stiffened momentarily; then he seemed to relax and suddenly slumped over in a heap. Rough, eager hands turned him over on his back and thrust themselves into his pockets; then one of the men pulled out Halliday's deed.

"Never mind, boys," he told them. "I got it."

His companions looked up.

"Yuh shore, Jess?"

"'Course I am," the latter snapped. He unfolded the deed. "Here. See that red thing in th' corner? That's a seal. That's what makes it legal. Savvy?"

"Uh-huh," another man said. "Y'know, that doggoned Halliday feller shore tried t' make things tough's he could f'r us, right down to th' end, didn't he? He musta chucked th' deed away hopin' that th' wind'd carry it off where we'd never find it. Lucky f'r us this hombre found it, eh?"

The man named Jess grunted in agreement.

"An' how," he said. "He shore saved us th' trouble o' huntin' f'r it in th' dark. Let's get goin'."

"What about this feller—this sleepin' beauty?"

"The hell with 'im," Jess answered quickly. "He don't know what we look like. He didn't get a chance t' see us. C'mon—let's get outta here b'fore someb'dy else comes along."

"Whatever yuh say, Jess," a man said. "On'y I figger yuh oughta put this feller outta th' way. He might talk, y'know—an' there's allus folks who'll listen."

Jess made no reply. He strode away. The other men followed. Presently the clatter of horses' hoofs arose, swelled briefly, then faded away completely. The black trotted forward again, pulled up beside Marshall and nudged him. Marshall stirred slightly and groaned. The big horse snorted impatiently and nudged him again, caught the rope that encircled Marshall with his teeth and jerked it savagely. It came away with surprisingly little resistance. Marshall stirred again, blinked and opened his eyes and groaned even louder than before.

"My head," he mumbled. "Oh—my head."

His right hand, free of the lariat, made its somewhat uncertain way up to his head. He touched it tenderly, gingerly. He struggled to sit up, fought for breath and strength, but the effort left him weak and limp and he sank down. Minutes later he tried again, forced himself up, bit by bit, and propped himself up on his elbows. The big horse watching with human understanding backed away and came up behind him and pushed him up into a sitting position. Marshall turned and groped blindly for the bridle. It was there, within easy reach too, and he gripped it tightly and dragged himself to his feet.

For a few fleeting minutes he clung grimly to the black, husbanding his slowly returning strength, drinking in the cool, crisp night air that bathed his face and eased his throbbing head. Finally he managed to get one foot into a stirrup, let go of the reins, clutched the saddle-horn with both hands and pulled himself up. He sank into the saddle with a groan. The black plodded away.

Marshall suddenly remembered the deed to the Halliday ranch. He plunged his hand into his jacket pocket and cursed aloud when he found it empty. So that was it. He had been waylaid for the deed. It was that clear and simple to understand. Obviously the men who had killed Halliday had "jumped" him. They had probably taken cover upon his approach, interrupted in their attempt to get the rancher's deed, waylaid him, removed the deed from his pocket and left him

11

there unconscious. The fact that he hadn't even caught a glimpse of his attackers was the reason for his being alive.

Anger and resentment flared up within him. He had been manhandled, and he objected to that. Then too there were other things that disturbed him, impersonal things of course—the murder, the theft of the deed—things that whetted his curiosity. His face grew hard and grim. He reached for the reins again, gripped them with a vengeance and settled himself more firmly in the saddle. The throb and the dull, pounding pain in his head were still present, but he disregarded them. His right hand dropped to his holster. The big Colt was there. He shifted the reins and felt for its mate. Yes, it was there too.

CHAPTER 2

IT WAS SATURDAY night and the town throbbed with activity and excitement. Of course there was always a wave of excitement when the cowpunchers from the neighboring ranches rode in from the range. But this was no ordinary, run-of-the-mill Saturday night with nothing to distinguish it from other Saturday nights. This was the all-important last Saturday of the month, and it bore the crowning significance that attached itself to payday.

The town's only street was thronged with money-laden punchers, pleasure bent and eager for excitement and entertainment. Noisy, boisterous, carefree, sun-tanned men with the unmistakable swaggering gait of horsemen, they overran the street, hailing their friends and the men from the other ranches with loud yells and ear-splitting whoops that would have done credit to bloodthirsty Comanches.

The town's stores, from one end of the street to the other, were ablaze with light, and many of them were already jammed with prospective purchasers who clamored loudly to be waited upon so that they could be on their way again to attend to more important and certainly more enjoyable "business."

Despite the fact that most of the store windows were dirty and mud-streaked, the result of a storm of some months before, the light managed to filter through to cast a yellowish gleam over the narrow wooden sidewalks and uneven curb and part way across the wheel-rutted gutter.

In the open doorways of the saloons which featured "girlie" shows, rouged, hard-faced women with brightly tinted shawls draped around them took up their posts. It was up to them to attract customers and get them to enter. Once they were inside, other women would take them over and, after joining them in a drink or two, would persuade them to try their luck at faro or at poker. The honey-tongued women usually experienced little difficulty in completing their work.

The pullers-in sized up each passerby with experienced, appraising eyes, singled out the likeliest-looking prospects and smiled at them and invited them to enter and partake of some entertainment. Some of the men accepted. Here and there a woman recognized a passing puncher and hailed him by name.

"Howdy, Rose," a broad-shouldered youth called.

The woman turned quickly.

"Hello, Handsome!" she said quickly with a warm smile. "What's the rush? Aren't you coming in? I've been saving something extra special for you."

The youth halted and grinned.

"Yeah? What?"

She gave him a seductive, sidelong glance.

"You don't want me to tell you out here, do you?" she asked in a low, coaxing voice that was too hard to be coy.

"N-o," the youth said slowly. "I s'pose not."

"Well?"

"I'm shore sorry, Rose. I'm busted. Just bought me a new saddle an' gun."

Rose's lips thinned.

"Huh!" she snapped scornfully. "You tinhorn! That's what I get for wasting my time on a cheapskate! A saddle and gun, eh? G'wan, you—you—!"

The puncher grinned sheepishly, circled around her and strode off. Rose gave her shawl a vicious jerk, glared after him and mumbled something under her breath. But in another moment her resentment at having lost out to a saddle and gun vanished. Another man sauntered along and glanced at her, running his eyes over her shawl-draped figure. Rose turned at that moment. He raised his eyes to meet hers.

"Oh, hello, Big Boy," she said, flashing her warmest smile.

The man smiled a bit in return and shuffled to a rather hesitant and consequently awkward halt in front of her.

"Howdy," he said presently, and waited.

Rose opened her shawl and settled it around her again, but she saw to it that he got a tempting and inviting flash of her bared shoulder and of a strip of satiny ribbon. Of course she pretended to be somewhat embarrassed when she looked up and found his probing eyes upon her, but when she glimpsed the expression on his face she discarded the pretense. She knew that he was "sold." She came directly to the point.

"Buy me a drink?" she asked.

The man grinned easily.

"Shore," he answered promptly.

Rose slid her arm through his.

"Let's go," she said cheerily. "Lil' Rosie's dry as a bone."

He laughed, and she squeezed his arm. They stepped into the saloon. Another girl, a younger one with a bright ribbon around her hair, came forward to meet them, but Rose caught her eye and shook her head vigorously. The girl smiled fleetingly, a smile of understanding, shrugged one slim shoulder and turned away. Rose led the man toward the bar, then reconsidered, changed her course midway across the floor and guided him toward a corner table. Two men were seated at the table toying with half emptied glasses of whisky in front of them. They looked up questioningly when Rose and her companion came up to them.

"Sorry, Boys," she said calmly, "but this table's r'served."

The two men looked at each other. One of them shrugged and climbed to his feet.

"Looks like we're in th' right church," he said with a grin, "but in th' wrong pew. C'mon, Matt—there's plenty o' room over at th' bar."

He turned away. The second man pushed his chair back from the table, arose and followed his companion away toward the bar. Rose and the man with her seated themselves. The man named Matt returned to the table.

"Forgot somethin'," he said. He reached over the table, picked up the half emptied glasses and drained them, one at a time, then set them down again. "Thanks."

He turned on his heel and strode off. Rose's lips thinned.

14

"Cheapskate," she said scornfully.

A waiter aproached and placed an uncorked bottle in front of them, then brought them two glasses. Rose's eyes brightened. She reached for the bottle, filled her companion's glass, then her own, and put down the bottle. She raised her glass. The man watched her, a smile of amusement on his face.

"Here's mud in your eye," she said brightly, smiled and drained her glass.

The man laughed lightly, swallowed his own drink and nodded toward the bottle. Rose reached for it again eagerly.

A splintered sign board that hung by a single nail from a wobbly post driven into the ground at the entrance to town claimed Marshall's attention. He edged his mount closer, leaned down from the saddle and studied the faded lettering on the board, shifted about until the moonlight came down over his shoulder and made reading less difficult.

"P-A-R-A-D-I-S-E." He read each letter aloud. "So this is Paradise, eh?"

He straightened up in the saddle and looked along the street that spread away in front of him. He eyed the milling, jostling cowpunchers for a minute.

"Never figgered it'd be so lively in Paradise," he muttered. "First I ever knew that angels sported silk shirts an' six-guns."

He nudged the black with his knees, and the big horse went on again. Midway along the street was a brightly lighted saloon. It appeared to be the busiest establishment in town. Marshall slowed the black when they came abreast of the place and looked in.

"Shore do a land-office bus'ness in there," he said half aloud. Then the name on the dirty window brought a grin to his face. "Angels' Cafe. Someb'dy 'round here's got a sense o' humor. Prob'bly needs it, too."

On the opposite side of the street a sign over a small, dimly lighted store window read "Sheriff." Marshall wheeled the black, guided him over to the curb, pulled up and dismounted. He hitched up his sagging gun belt, looked around casually and was sauntering across the sidewalk toward the door when it opened suddenly and four men filed out. Marshall came to an abrupt halt. The men glanced at him and brushed past him.

15

He went on again. The door was ajar, and he pushed it open and halted in the doorway. Behind a battered desk in the middle of the room sat a burly man with thin, greying hair. He looked up.

"Yeah?" he asked.

"You th' Sheriff?" Marshall asked.

"That's what th' sign outside says, don't it?"

Marshall did not reply. He turned instead and closed the door. The burly man eyed him appraisingly and waited. Marshall faced him again presently.

"Found a dead man on th' trail comin' in," he began. "Figgered you'd wanna know 'bout it right off."

The Sheriff grunted.

"Awright. Where'bouts was it?"

"Oh—'bout two hours' ride fr'm here, I'd say."

"Go on."

Marshall sauntered forward. There were some papers on the desk, and the Sheriff reached for them hastily and turned them face downward. Marshall pretended not to notice. He halted in front of the desk, pushed his hat back from his eyes, and glanced around the office. There was a chair in a far corner of the room, and he turned and strode over, picked it up and carried it back and put it down near the desk.

"Make y'self comf'table," the Sheriff said dryly.

"Oh, thanks," Marshall said, and seated himself. He looked up. "This feller I was tellin' yuh 'bout had a bullet hole right smack b'tween th' eyes."

"Uh-huh. Find 'nything on 'im?"

The black-clad man smiled coldly.

"Didn't look. Picked up a piece o' paper in 'mongst some brush just past th' spot where he was layin'. Th' paper was a deed to a ranch."

The Sheriff's face was expressionless and gave no inkling of his thoughts. His eyes never left Marshall's face.

"What was th' name on th' deed?" he asked.

"Halliday—Jim Halliday."

The Sheriff shifted himself in his chair. It creaked protestingly under his weight.

"This here deed yuh found—" he began presently—"let's have a look at it."

"Haven't got it," Marshall said quietly.

16

The burly man's eyebrows arched.

"Yuh haven't, eh? What'd yuh do with it?"

Marshall settled back in his chair.

"Couple o' fellers jumped me," he replied. "They took th' danged thing."

The Sheriff frowned. He leaned forward and rested his heavy arms on the desk and stared at Marshall. He was evidently weighing Marshall's story by puzzling over it.

"I s'pose yuh c'n tell me what those fellers looked like, eh?" he asked presently.

Marshall shook his head.

"Nope," he said. "It was dark, an' it all happened so sudden-like that even now I dunno how many there were o' them. 'Course I tried to fight 'em off, but it was no go. Then someb'dy walloped me over th' head an' laid me out cold."

"An' when yuh come to," the Sheriff added, "they were gone an' so was th' deed. Right?"

"That's th' way it was."

The Sheriff jerked open a desk drawer, fumbled with some papers, pulled out a folded sheet and tossed it on the desk.

"That th' deed yuh're talkin' 'bout?" he demanded.

Marshall reached for the paper, picked it up and unfolded it. He glanced at it; then a frown darkened his face. He eyed the Sheriff sharply.

"This is it, awright. S'pose yuh tell me how you got hold of it?"

"I aim to, Mister," the Sheriff said coldly.

He pushed his chair away from the desk, climbed to his feet and trudged to the door and threw it open.

"Jess!" he roared. "C'm'in here!"

Marshall heard a heavy step, a shuffling of feet; then four men crowded past the Sheriff and into the office. The Sheriff shouldered his way through them and plodded back to his chair. Marshall eyed the newcomers. He recognized them at once. They were the four men he had seen filing out of the office as he had walked toward it. He sensed at once that he had stumbled into something that he hadn't bargained for. But he held his tongue and waited. He would know what it was all about soon enough.

"Mister," he heard the Sheriff say, "ever see any o' these men b'fore?"

Marshall's eyes swept over the four men again.

"Dunno," he replied. "Why d'yuh ask?"

The Sheriff disregarded Marshall's question.

"Jess," he said loudly.

A tall, lean man, his thumbs hooked in his heavy gun belt, looked up.

"Yeah, Sam?"

"Jess," the Sheriff asked, "you ever see this hombre b'fore?"

Jess laughed lightly.

"Shore."

"How 'bout you other fellers?" the Sheriff demanded. "He look f'miliar to yuh?"

The other three men sauntered forward, glanced at Marshall as they passed him and halted, hands on hips, one of them a few feet behind him, the others on either side of him.

"Wa-al?" the Sheriff demanded impatiently. "How 'bout it?"

The three men nodded in unison.

"Reckon that settles it awright," the Sheriff said. He looked at Marshall again. "Mister, yuh asked me b'fore how I come to have that there deed. F'r yore inf'rmation, Jess an' his men here brung it to me."

Marshall's eyes gleamed.

"They did, eh? Then they're th' polecats who jumped me," he retorted. He eyed Jess sharply. "Reckon that coyote's th' one who walloped me over th' head."

Jess grinned easily.

"Uh-huh. I walloped yuh when yuh were tryin' to escape," he said calmly.

"Yuh're a liar," Marshall snapped. "An' while I'm about it, I'm willin' to go on record an' charge you an' yore hellions with killin' this Halliday, too."

Jess laughed.

"Go 'head. Nob'dy payin' any attention to yuh an' yore charges," he replied. He turned to the Sheriff. "Get this over with, Sam."

The Sheriff cleared his throat.

"Mister," he began, "I had Jess an' th' boys come in t' see if they could identify yuh. Fr'm th' way they all identified yuh as th' feller they seen trailin' Halliday, it shore looks like they got yuh dead t' rights. Accordin' to them, an' th' word o' four o' them 'gainst yourn, they heard yuh shoot an' come

18

'pon yuh rifling Halliday's pockets. They cornered yuh, but yuh managed to get away after a scrap. In yore hurry yuh dropped Jim's deed. Wa-al, I reckon that about winds things up. I'm holdin' yuh f'r murder. Take his guns, Boys!"

CHAPTER 3

MARSHALL, TENSED and poised for action, had already planned what he would do. He had no intention of submitting meekly, despite the odds against him, certain that it was all part of a crudely conceived plot in which he, a stranger, was to be "sacrificed" to cover up Jess and his men. Instinctively he sensed that the man behind him would make the first move to disarm him. That he had anticipated the move correctly was immediately evident, for the man stepped forward and reached for the brace of heavy black Colts which hung low against Marshall's thighs. It was evident too that the man had given no thought to the possibility that Marshall might resist, for he proceeded in a most unguarded manner. Marshall, readying himself for a move of his own, shifted a bit.

"Stand still," the man growled.

His fingers touched the butt of one gun. Marshall drove his elbow into the man's face and heard him cry out. Without a moment's delay he whirled and lunged for the man on his left. The latter, totally unprepared to defend himself against a sudden attack, was taken by surprise, and his instinctive resistance, which consisted of a hastily thrown up right arm with which to ward off his attacker, was brushed aside by the suddenness and the viciousness of Marshall's lunge.

Marshall clamped his left arm around the man's neck, tightened the vise in a flash, whirled him around, using him as a shield against possible gunfire, and dragged him back while his free right hand streaked toward his holster.

"Leggo!" the man gasped. "Leggo, willya!"

Marshall's gun cleared its holster. He swung it up and snapped a lightning shot over his unwilling captive's shoulder at the swinging lamp that hung from the ceiling. The bullet found its mark, shattered the lamp and sent it plummeting to the floor, where it crashed with deafening, ear-splitting thunder and burst into a thousand pieces. The office was instantly plunged into darkness.

Marshall clubbed the struggling man over the head with his gun. The captive collapsed in Marshall's arms. He shoved him away hard, and heard him strike the floor. He wheeled and plunged headlong for the desk, seeking momentary safety behind it, collided midway with the very chair he had been using but minutes before, caught it up and swung it aloft and hurled it across the darkened room. The cry of pain that followed told him that it had struck someone, and he judged that it was the third of Jess' henchmen who had felt his wrath.

"Kill th' murderin' dog!" he heard Jess roar.

Guns crashed and flame stabbed the darkness. Man-made thunder rocked the building. The floor creaked dismally on the opposite side of the desk. It was the Sheriff plunging blindly and with reckless abandon toward the open door. Marshall whirled around the desk in pursuit. Just as the Sheriff reached the door, a thunderbolt struck him, staggered him, threw him off balance and sent him stumbling awkwardly, full tilt, into Jess. Both men crashed heavily to the floor.

Marsall burst through the open door and into the moonlit street, whirled in his tracks and emptied his gun into the darkened office. A voice cried out in pain. A man staggered to the door and fell against the door jamb, straightened up and stumbled across the threshold, halted there on unsteady, buckling legs and suddenly sagged in his tracks and sank down. He huddled in the doorway for a moment; then he simply toppled over, blocking it with his sprawled body. Marshall dashed to the curb, vaulted into the saddle and drove his spurs into the black's flanks. The big horse bounded away as though he had been catapulted through space.

In a twinkling the street was filled with curious, eager-eyed men, attracted by the crash of guns.

"What is it?" someone demanded excitedly. "What's goin' on?"

"Dunno," another man replied. "Must be someb'dy celebratin'."

"Celebratin' hell!" a third man snapped. "Some feller on a

big horse just went past here like a bat outta hell. There he is now—see? Nearin' th' corner."

"Look!" still another man cried. "Ain't that someb'dy layin' in th' doorway o' th' Sheriff's office?"

"It shore is!" a voice answered. "Hey! That feller musta shot up th' place! C'm'on!"

A dozen men darted across the street. Two of them, youthful and excited, halted in the middle of the gutter, yanked out their guns and snapped a couple of shots in the general direction of the fleeting black.

"C'm'on, yuh danged fools!" and older man gritted over his shoulder. "Yuh might's well try t' drill a ghost as that feller. He's travelin' 'bout even with th' wind, an' that's a heap faster'n lead!"

From the doorway of a darkened shack a barefooted man clad in long underwear blazed away at the phantom target with a heavy buffalo gun which boomed with the deep-throated rumble of distant thunder. From other points along the street Winchesters and six-guns opened fire, too, adding their voices to the already mounting din, but it was hurried, inaccurate and uncertain shooting, and the results were completely negative.

Far down the moonlit street, at the very corner where the street ended and the widespreading range began, a group of men appeared in the open doorway of a saloon just as the black came abreast of the place.

"Hey!" one of the men yelled.

He shouldered his way through his hesitant mates and plunged out, gun in hand. A couple of his companions joined him presently. When he raised his gun, they did, too. A blast of gunfire whined around Marshall, who had thrown himself forward against his mount's neck. He jerked the black to a dust-raising halt, whirled him around and pulled out one of his Colts.

"Why, yuh danged polecats!" he yelled angrily. "Awright— if that's th' way yuh want it—here!"

Flame belched from his gun. One of the saloon's two windows fell out with a deafening crash, showering the men in front of the place with bits of glass. Most of them scampered away hastily, all save one man, the man who had yelled at Marshall. This man, more determined than his mates, stepped

21

to the curb and fired twice at Marshall. The heavy Colt swept downward—both men fired at the same time.

The man at the curb dropped his gun, turned slowly and toppled over in a heap.

Marshall holstered his gun, wheeled the black and loped away. He twisted around once and looked back, settled himself again presently in the saddle, guided the big horse northward and disappeared into the night.

A crowd of excited men gathered in front of the Sheriff's darkened office. The limp body in the doorway was dragged out, and now it lay sprawled out on the sidewalk with a circle of men around it.

"It's Jerry Dawson!" a man said.

"Doggone if it ain't!" another said.

Sam Barnes appeared in the doorway.

"There's th' Sheriff now!"

Everyone looked up.

"Hey, Sam—" a man began.

The Sheriff stumbled out, pushed past him, made his way to the curb and sat down heavily. Jess Barnes emerged now, too.

"Get yore horses, men!" he cried. "We're goin' after that murderin' polecat an' hang 'im t' th' first tree we c'n find! C'm'on— make it lively now!"

"Just a minute, Barnes!" a tall man called. "What happened in there? What was all th' shootin' about?"

"That maverick that just hightailed it away fr'm here murdered Jim Halliday," Jess answered.

"Why, th' dirty dog!"

"Me an' th' boys chased 'im," Jess continued quickly, "but he got away fr'm us. While we were tryin' t' pick up his trail again, he makes a beeline f'r town, heads f'r th' Sheriff's office an' r'ports that he found a dead man on th' trail in an'—"

"Th' gall o' th' critter!" a man said angrily.

"We come 'long just when he's finishin' this yarn o' his," Jess went on. "Soon's he seen us he went f'r 'is guns an'—"

The tall man interrupted with an impatient gesture.

"Yuh say he murdered Jim Halliday, eh?" he demanded.

"That's right, Davis. Yuh c'n ask th' boys if yuh wanna. They'll tell yuh, awright."

"H'm," Davis muttered. He looked down at the motionless

22

figure on the sidewalk. "That some o' that hellion's work, too?"

Jess nodded.

"Yep," he answered grimly. "He got th' drop on us. Jerry tried t' stop 'im fr'm gettin' away, but he didn't have a chance. He wasn't fast enough on th' draw."

"Looks like this hombre an' his horse are 'bout even when it comes t' speed," Davis remarked.

A bystander nudged him.

"He shot 'nother feller," the man said quickly, excitedly, "down th' street a ways. Yuh c'n see 'im fr'm here—layin' on th' sidewalk near th' curb."

There was a general turning and a craning of necks. The tall man squared his shoulders, and shifted his holster a bit.

"We-ll," he said with finality, "if we aim to catch up with this killer, we'd better quit jawin' an' start ridin'. Just gimme a minute to get m' horse an' I'll be with yuh."

He wheeled and shouldered his way out of the crowd and strode off. A dozen or more men in the crowd, evidently taking their cue from him, scurried away, too. They returned minutes later, some of them already mounted and carrying their rifles, others leading their horses by their bridles. Jess Barnes, astride his horse, was waiting for them.

"Yuh all set?" he demanded, impatience in his tone.

"Shore," a dozen voices answered promptly. "Someb'dy got a rope?"

"Here y'are," a man said loudly. He jerked a lariat off his saddlehorn and held it aloft. "It ain't new, but I reckon it'll do awright."

"I got one," Jess said. "It's bran'-new an' just beggin' t' be used."

Davis came riding up to him.

"Awright, Barnes," he said. "Whenever yuh're ready."

Jess nodded.

"Soon's Sam gets his horse," he answered.

More men rode up, swelling the ranks of the posse to more than twenty. The Sheriff appeared presently, astride a big white horse. Jess looked at him and frowned.

"Take yore time, Sam," he said coldly, through his teeth. "We got all th' time in th' world y'know. Like's not that

23

maverick's settin' down some place just waitin' f'r us t' come an' get him."

The Sheriff made no reply, but the expression on his heavy face bespoke his feelings in the matter. It was evident that he did not relish the prospect of an all-night ride when he could, effortlessly and with complete comfort, spend the night in town. It would be cold on the range; the wind that swept into town from the open prairie was sharp and chilling.

"C'm'on," Jess said curtly.

He wheeled his mount. The Sheriff followed him to the head of the party. Jess glanced at him, stood up in his stirrups and looked back over the waiting cavalcade.

"Awright!" he cried. "Let's go!"

He spurred his horse and sent him racing away. The Sheriff and the rest of the posse followed, strung out behind him in little bands of two's and three's. The clatter of pounding hoofs filled the air as the horsemen swept down the street. The women poured out from the now deserted saloons and lined the curb. They watched with expressions of disgust on their faces.

"That's that," one woman said. "We might as well call it a day and turn in."

The woman on her right nodded.

" 'Course. They won't be back t'night any more," she added.

"Who—who are they going after?" a younger voice asked.

Rose sauntered out, her shawl draped lightly over one shoulder, the other bared to the cool night air. She opened her shawl quickly and gathered it around her.

"Who?" she echoed. "Oh, prob'bly some fool who got drunk and picked a fight with another drunk. It always starts that way. First thing you know there's some gun play and somebody gets hurt or killed, and the one who started the thing sobers up in an awful hurry and hightails it away. Then they get a posse together and they go after 'im. Come on, girls— let's go back inside. It's cold out here. Come on—we can all stand a drink."

The party of horsemen was now nearing the corner. Jess, far out in front of the others, swung his mount northward. It was evidently his belief that the fugitive would seek safety in the hills. The other horsemen followed Jess' lead. They lashed their mounts and urged them on in an effort to close up the gap between him and themselves.

24

CHAPTER 4

IT WAS MID-MORNING of the following day. The sun was bright and strong. It sifted through the gaps in the ragged and faded window blind and flooded the Sheriff's office with light. Bright, capering rays darted over the ceiling and walls and over the battered desk in the middle of the room. On the floor in front of the desk was a thick, blackened, greasy splotch, the remains of the oil from the shattered lamp. It glistened brightly when a ray of light focused upon it.

Jess Barnes was lounging in a chair near the desk. He turned his head and blinked in the strong sunlight, shading his eyes with his hand. Finally he arose, stepped over the oil splotch, strode to the window and reached for the blind. He seemed annoyed when he found that it had been torn in half and that the lower half was gone. He muttered something to himself, turned on his heel and retraced his steps, circling the oil stain this time instead of stepping over it. He caught up his chair, swung it around and seated himself again with his back to the window. He shifted himself until he was comfortable, or as comfortable as the hard, straight-backed chair permitted him to be, and glanced at the Sheriff, who was lounging in his own chair behind the desk, staring off into space. Jess rubbed his chin reflectively, debated something with himself, then, his mind evidently made up, swung around again.

"Sam," he said.

"Huh?" The Sheriff jerked his head up. "Yuh say somethin'?"

Jess examined a callus in the palm of his hand.

"Sam," he said again without looking up, "I'm takin' over th' Halliday place."

The Sheriff gulped and swallowed hard.

"Yuh're what?"

Jess looked up. Their eyes met.

"What's th' matter—yuh gone deaf all of a sudden?" Jess demanded. "I said I'm takin' over th' Halliday place."

"That's what I thought yuh said."

Jess gave him a baleful glare.

"Well?" he demanded.

Sam swung around in his chair. It creaked under his weight.

"Doggone it," he sputtered. "Doggone it anyway, Jess—yuh know yuh can't do that."

Jess smiled coldly.

"No? Who says I can't?"

"Who?" the Sheriff echoed. "Why, th' law—that's who. Yuh know danged well, Jess Barnes, that I can't just hand it over to yuh. Th' law says I gotta put th' place up f'r public sale."

"Awright. Yuh just put it up f'r sale—an' I bought it."

Sam grunted.

"Yuh don't say? Mebbe yuh'd like t' tell me what yuh paid f'r it?" he said, a trace of sarcasm in his voice.

Jess pretended not to notice it. He grinned instead and shrugged his shoulder.

"Can't 'cause I dunno f'r shore—yet," he replied. "S'pose you put a price on it."

"Me? How'n hell can I? What do I know 'bout a ranch or what one's worth?" the Sheriff demanded. "Shucks, far's I'm c'ncerned Halliday's place ain't worth a cent."

"Awright. That's what I'm payin' f'r it."

Sam stared hard at him.

"Yuh gone loco? Yuh musta—else yuh're just foolin'."

"I ain't—neither one. Get out that there Halliday deed." Jess commanded.

"Now, Jess . . ."

"You heard me."

"Doggone it, Jess," the Sheriff sputtered again. "Yuh can't get away with that kinda thing, an' yuh know it. What'll folks think when they hear of it? First thing yuh know someb'dy'll say there's some c'nnection b'tween Halliday's bein' murdered an' you grabbin' off his ranch."

"An' what'll be th' next thing?"

Sam snorted loudly.

"Someb'dy'll just say you must be th' feller that murdered Jim," he said quickly. "An' won't that be somethin'?"

Jess leaned forward in his chair.

"Th' hell with 'em. Let 'em say anythin' they like. They ain't th' law. Yuh're the law, Sam," he said quietly. "Yuh're th'

26

on'y one who c'n do anythin' about it, an' yuh won't, will yuh, Sam?"

"Wa-al—"

"Sam," Jess went on, "you don't think I had 'nything t' do with Jim Halliday's killin', do yuh? You don't think I killed 'im, do yuh?"

An expression of surprise swept over the Sheriff's face.

"Heck, no," he answered. "Yuh told me that that danged killer done it, an' I just took yore word f'r it. Why, I never even thought o' doubtin' yuh, Jess—not f'r even a minute."

Jess smiled amiably.

"'Course not," he said. "Yuh're awright, Sam. Yuh're plenty awright. I've allus said so, ain't I? Now go 'head, Sam—fix up that there deed f'r me an' let's have it done with."

"Shore, Jess, right away," Sam said. Then a frown darkened his heavy face. "Just a minute. We gotta do somethin' 'bout th' price, y'know."

"What—we goin' over that again?" Jess laughed and got to his feet. He leaned over the desk and patted the Sheriff's shoulder. "S'pose yuh leave that t' me, Sam? Ol' Jess ain't gonna let yuh down. Heck, you oughta know that. I'll fix up everything. You got nuthin' t' worry 'bout. Now dig up th' deed like a good feller, will yuh?"

He straightened up. The Sheriff dug into the mass of papers on his desk, fumbled among them for a minute, then stopped abruptly and slowly looked up. Jess eyed him questioningly.

"What's th' matter now?" he asked.

Sam gulped again.

"Th' deed," he said falteringly. "It—it ain't here."

The smile on Jess' face—it wasn't more than a trace of a smile now—vanished.

"It ain't, eh?" Jess mused.

His face was suddenly hard and grim. His lips curled wolfishly, baring his teeth. His arm shot out. He grabbed Sam by the shirt-front and dragged him out of his chair.

"Listen t' me, Sam," he said thickly. "If yuh're tryin' t' play smart now, don't. I'll give yuh th' same's I gave—well, don't, that's all."

Sam blinked, but Jess did not release his grip.

"Well?" he demanded gruffly.

"Doggone it, Jess," the Sheriff began. "Yuh got no call t'

27

act thataway with me. Yuh oughta know I wouldn't try 'ny tricks on you. Heck, I'm yore brother, ain't I, an' older'n you are?"

Jess smiled coldly.

"Yeah, m' half-brother but that don't make 'ny diff'rence t' me. Cross me an' I'll fix yuh good—understan'? Yuh gonna do like I tell yuh or not?"

Sam tried to nod.

"'Course I am, Jess," he said as quickly and as convincingly as he could.

"That's better." Jess released him. "Now what about that deed?"

"That—that feller had it in his hand when you an' th' boys come in," Sam explained hopefully. "I don't r'member what b'come of it after that—things happened so fast, y'know."

"Then he got away with it, eh?"

"Uh-huh. So y' see, there's nuthin' I c'n do 'bout it now. If we'da caught 'im, we coulda crossed out Jim Halliday's name an' put in yourn," the Sheriff went on eagerly. "Aw, what th' heck, Jess—Halliday's place ain't so much. You'll find another one that'll be even better. Mebbe heaps better, too. You'll see."

Jess Barnes' eyes glinted.

"Shut up," he said gruffly. "Sit down there an' write out a hull new deed an' make it out in my name."

Sam's eyes widened.

"Now, Jess—"

"Do's I tell yuh!"

The Sheriff shook his head sorrowfully.

"Get outta th' way," Jess said curtly.

He came around the desk and shouldered Sam out of the way. He yanked open the middle drawer, found a legal form and pulled it out. He glanced at it, smiled and nodded to himself. There was a stub of a pencil on the desk, and he picked it up and scribbled his name on the line above the caption "Owner's Name." He tossed the pencil on the desk.

"There y' are. Sign it."

"Awright, Jess, if I gotta. What about where it says 'how much'?" he asked.

Jess looked up at him.

"How much, eh?" he repeated. He dug into his pants' pocket,

drew out a silver dollar and tossed it on the desk. "There y'are —one dollar."

"Looka here, Jess. . . ."

"Sign it!"

When Sam hesitated, Jess' right hand dropped swiftly to his holster. The Sheriff's eyes followed Jess' hand, saw his fingers tighten around his gun butt.

"Well?"

Sam sighed, picked up the pencil, drew the deed to him and scratched his name on it. Jess pushed him away, picked up the paper, folded it and shoved it into his pocket. He climbed to his feet.

"That's that. Now lemme tell yuh somethin'."

The Sheriff raised his eyes. There was an expression of helplessness on his face, resignation in his manner.

"That other feller didn't kill Halliday," Jess said calmly. He smiled coldly. "I did."

Sam Barnes' eyes widened. He gulped, and his lips twitched a couple of times, for a fleeting instant each time, but no sound came from him. He seemed to be gripped by something that permitted his senses of hearing and understanding to function, but that rendered him incapable of speech. All he could do was stare and gulp.

"T' make it look good, an' t' leave me in th' clear," Jess went on in a tantalizingly even tone of voice, "yuh're gonna go on lookin' f'r that hombre. Yuh're bound t' catch up with 'im sooner or later, an' when yuh do—if yuh're smart an' if yuh wanna go on livin' off th' fat o' th' land like yuh're doin' now—yuh'll shoot first an' shoot t' kill. 'Course if yuh don't get th' chance to—well, then yuh better see to it that someb'dy uses a rope on 'im—on 'is neck."

There was no comment from Sam—nothing but a wide-eyed stare.

"Outside o' m' own men—an' I know they ain't th' talkin' kind—an' you, Sam, nob'dy else knows that I had 'nything t' do with Halliday's killin'. If anyb'dy else finds it out—well, I'll know who told 'em. I don't hafta tell yuh what'll happen to yuh then, do I?"

Sam gulped again. Jess smiled. patted his holster significantly, wheeled and started toward the door, only to halt for a moment and give Sam a quick backward glance over his shoulder, before he went on again and strode out. The door slammed loudly behind him, but the Sheriff failed to notice it. He stumbled blindly toward his chair, reached it finally and sank into it heavily.

CHAPTER 5

THE HALLIDAY PLACE—it was usually referred to as the Bar JH—was in reality an island ranch.

A low, sturdy, sprawling ranchhouse, strong, solidly built to withstand time and attack—it might well have been a manor house had one been willing to overlook the fact that it lacked both battlements and parapets—stood atop a knoll in the very center of the Bar JH.

A moat that was some thirty feet wide encircled the island ranch on the south and on the east and separated it from the mainland proper. To the north were tall, towering, majestic mountains, a nature-made wall that stood between the Bar JH and the outside world. To round out the picture, a bridge spanned the deep moat—not a drawbridge such as one might have expected to find there, but a crude, sturdy structure of logs, a bridge that was strong enough to support the weight of a heavily laden farm wagon and a sweating, panting four-horse team. Often the bridge had echoed with the thumping, vibrating tread of milling cattle; sometimes, too, fleet, wiry cow ponies had flashed over it.

A swirling, noisy, treacherous river with a deadly undertow midstream—Thunder River the Indians had named it—spun southward past the Bar JH. The flow began in some hidden caves in the mountains; from a point high up in the mountains a waterfall shot outward and hurtled downward through space until it plunged into the river below with a thunderous roar that was both deafening and terrifying.

The sharp metallic ring of a cantering horse's hoofs echoed through the morning air. The clatter of iron-shod hoofs on a straightaway stretch of hard, stony ground swelled briefly as the horse approached, then faded out abruptly as the horse burst into view and halted atop a steep trail.

One might have looked up and stared at the horse, but only until one realized that the horse was not riderless and that its rider was a girl. Realization would have caused one's eyes to widen to encompass them both, for together they made an eye-filling picture that was part golden mare and part—well, one promptly forgot about the mare and eyed the girl alone interestedly.

The girl was pretty, even at a distance, in spite of her completely mannish attire that included a pair of ordinary but thoroughly masculine boots, rough flannel work shirt and overalls. She was a graceful figure; one knew at once from the way she sat her horse that she had lived much of her life in the saddle.

The mare pawed the ground once, impatiently, anxious to be moving on again, but the girl jerked the reins sharply and her mount subsided. She scanned the trail that dipped away below them, the open country that spread before their eyes; then she nudged the mare with her knees and the dainty-hoofed animal went on again, slowly, down the trail and onto level ground.

They halted again presently while the girl looked skyward. The early morning sun was bright and strong and dazzling. There was something of a haze on the distant horizon, a promise of a warm day. The mare whinnied, and the girl leaned forward and patted her mount's neck affectionately. They went on again in another minute, swerved away from the trail and rode slowly down a sloping, grassy incline and stopped finally when they came to a wall of thick brush.

The girl dismounted, tethered the mare and opened her saddle bag. It was a large and roomy affair, apparently filled to overflownig, judging by the difficulty she experienced in finding whatever it was that she sought. Finally, after a minute's rummaging through the bag's contents, she drew out a towel-wrapped object. Satisfied, she closed the saddle bag and stepped back.

"I won't be long, Honey," she said to her mount.

The mare turned her head and rubbed her nose against the girl's shoulder.

"Be a good girl."

31

Honey whinnied again, turned away, spied a patch of fresh young grass just beyond her that looked particularly inviting and tempting, eyed it for a moment, then edged her way forward to it and proceeded to munch it. The girl watched her, turned presently and trudged off into the brush. When she reappeared, towel in hand, she was barelegged and barefooted and clad in a short, sleeveless dress.

The dress was worn, faded and drab; she offset its dullness by the use of a bright ribbon with which she had bound up her hair.

Briskly she made her way to the water's edge, strode along the grassy bank till she came to two huge boulders that stood at the very edge and stepped between them. She was hidden from sight for a moment, her dress was suddenly whisked off and tossed onto one of the boulders, then a sharp splash followed.

A lithe figure flashed through the water, and a glistening, ribbon-bound head suddenly bobbed to the surface in the middle of the stream. She threw herself backwards and floated with the current, lazily, contentedly, for a moment, only to jerk herself upward again with startling suddenness when she heard a splash somewhere beyond her. Quickly she looked about her.

A hundred feet away, downstream, a man's head suddenly pushed its way up through the water; then his bared, glistening shoulders and arms appeared.

The girl screamed. They stared hard at each other for a brief moment; then both whirled about with equal suddenness and streaked away toward shore.

Marshall's flushed face wore a frown as he trudged up the bank. Dressing himself quickly he swung his gun belt around his waist, buckled it on viciously. He spied a broken twig on the ground just ahead of him, drew back his right foot and kicked it out of his path.

"Damnation," he muttered. "Can't even go f'r a swim at sunup without runnin' into someb'dy, an' of all people, a woman."

He shook his head sadly. Then the frown vanished suddenly, and his face relaxed. A boyish grin flickered over his mouth.

"Boy," he mused. "Did she holler! Doggone—bet I scared 'er out of a hull year's growth!"

He passed a clump of brush, and a slim figure, upraised gun in hand, whirled out behind him.

"Stand where you are!" a girl's voice commanded coldly. Marshall halted.

"Get your hands up!"

He grunted, and raised his hands skyward, slowly.

"Turn around!"

He obeyed, slowly as before. Anger and resentment began to well up within him. In another minute he'd forget that she was only a woman and—

His eyes widened—he was jolted by what he found confronting him. The girl was pretty—in fact, she was without doubt the prettiest thing he had ever seen. He stared at her, hating to take his eyes from her, but he did, finally, just long enough to glance at the gun in her steady hand and at the muzzle that gaped at him. Back his eyes shifted again, to her face, then to her hair. It was golden, just like a setting sun, and her angry eyes beneath it—well, he drew a deep breath as if it would have to last him a long time—they were soft and warm and blue as the evening sky.

"Who are you?" she demanded. "What are you doing here?"

He shook his head—a girl couldn't be so completely pretty as all that.

"Me? Oh. Name's Marshall, Ma'am."

"Thank you," she said coldly. "Do you always stare at people?"

He managed a sheepish grin.

"No, reckon not—leastways, I don't r'member doin' it b'fore. Mebbe that's b'cause I never saw a girl who was as pretty as you, Ma'am."

She averted her eyes for a moment.

"This is private property," she said presently, icily. "We don't like trespassers around here, and when we catch them we know how to deal with them. Now turn around and get out of here."

He shrugged his broad shoulders.

"Awright—if you say so."

He turned slowly, hitched up his belt and strode away toward the thicket. He pushed his way into it, disappeared with-

33

in it for a moment, and reappeared presently leading the black.

He made no attempt to look at the girl, although he knew she was still there, gun in hand, watching him, waiting for him to leave. He vaulted into the saddle, wheeled the big horse and cantered away.

The knoll looked down upon the heavy bridge that connected the Bar JH with the mainland.

The black plodded up the hill and halted gratefully when Marshall jerked the reins. It had been a long, hard, uphill ride —the hot sun overhead hadn't made the going any easier, either—and the big horse was winded and spent. Marshall dismounted and loosened the cinches.

"How's that?" he asked. "Better, ain't it?"

He patted the glistening, sweaty neck of his mount.

He sauntered forward a bit, almost to the very edge of the rise, and squatted down, cross-legged. From where he sat he could see the rough-hewn bridge, the approach to it over the rolling prairie, the moat and the curving shoreline of the island ranch. His eyes ranged over it, interestedly, westward to the river—swift and swirling and white-crested as it spun southward. Far to the north, rising majestically beyond the ranch itself, were towering mountains from which came a distant echo of booming, thundering falls.

A horseman came riding out of the ranch. Tall, thick-trunked, closely-packed trees ringed the island and thrust themselves high into the sky, forming a formidable barrier around the place, so completely so that it was impossible for anyone, even Marshall who was perched almost above it, to see into the Bar JH. The horseman drew rein near the bridge. He looked up quickly when he heard hoof beats. Marshall heard them too, faintly of course, and he shifted his gaze and followed the man's eyes.

Across the prairie came the girl, her mare's hoofs flashing over the turf at a swift, even gallop. Marshall eyed her sharply, a deepening frown on his face.

"H'm!" he grunted. "That's her, awright!"

There was annoyance and resentment in his tone—it was evident that she was going to turn up everywhere he went. He watched her for a moment, critically.

"She shore knows how t' ride," he muttered presently.

34

"Can't take that away fr'm 'er. Fr'm here yuh'd think she was part of 'er horse."

He shifted his eyes again, this time to the horseman. The man sat his mount quietly, motionlessly, waiting. The girl spied him now and checked her horse's pace; then she nudged the mare and sent her on again. The mare came clattering over the bridge.

Marshall half arose. There was something in the girl's actions that made him sense trouble. As he watched, he saw the man ride forward to meet the oncoming girl, saw her try to swerve away from him, but the man was too quick for her. He reached for her bridle. She attempted to pull away, but the man would not be denied. He caught the bridle in a desperate, reckless, lunging clutch that almost unseated him, pulled himself back into the saddle again instantly, jerked the reins viciously and brought the prancing mare to a stop. He swung his own mount around and ranged him alongside of her. From all immediate indications the struggle appeared to be over; probably it would have been if the man's horse hadn't bumped Honey and trod on her. The mare screamed, whirled like a cornered cat, reared up and lashed out at the other horse with flashing fore hoofs.

There was an exciting battle for a moment—a throwback to the primitive—with the two horses pitted against each other, kicking and trampling one another.

The girl, helpless and carried away by the swift action, suddenly twisted around in her saddle when the man's horse swept him close to her, swung her clenched fist and struck at him. It was a glancing blow, little more than an excitable gesture and a rather futile blow at that. That it had little effect on the man was evident, for he did not release or shift his grip on the bridle. But the blow seemed to spur the mare on. Frothing and panting and aroused, she leaped forward again as though she intended to bowl her opponent over.

Unfortunately there was insufficient room for a real charge. Actually it was close quarters, and Honey's frenzied rush died aborning. The man was ready for her, and drove his mount into her and forced her back. He shifted his grip on the reins suddenly in an upward sweep, gave them an equally sudden and vicious twist so that the iron bit cut deep into the mare's jaws. Honey cried out, and Marshall, watching from his lofty perch above them, was certain that the man laughed. Marshall's face grew hard and grim. He came erect now, mechanically.

The mare suddenly pulled away. The girl, evidently on the alert for an opportunity that offered even half a chance for escape, took full advantage of the situation. In a twinkling she had swung her left leg over the saddle horn; she dropped lightly to the ground, backed and turned in a single motion and fled. The man released the mare's bridle and whirled his horse around. The girl raced away toward the bridge.

"Come back here, dang yuh!" the man cried.

Marshall's hands tightened around the butts of his guns.

"Awright!" the man yelled. "Mebbe this'll learn yuh!"

A lariat suddenly appeared in his right hand. High over his head it twirled, the loop opening and widening in a great, graceful arc. He drew back his arm. A Colt roared overhead. Its thunder echoed over the range. The man's arm fell—the lariat collapsed in mid-air, slipped out of his hand, dropped harmlessly and limply to the ground. The man sagged a bit, and slumped forward in his saddle. The girl was across the bridge now and racing breathlessly for the open range.

Marshall turned quickly, holstering his gun. He reached the waiting black in a skidding dash, tightened the cinches with sure, swift hands, vaulted into the saddle and wheeled the big horse.

He stood up in the stirrups and peered over the edge of the knoll. The man below was swaying in his saddle. Slowly he wheeled his horse and rode off into the trees. The mare whinnied, turned and trotted after him. Marshall grunted and dropped down into his own saddle.

"Awright!" he said curtly.

The black cantered away.

"Wa-al?" Marshall demanded. "What's keepin' yuh?"

The big horse snorted and quickened his pace.

CHAPTER 6

THE GIRL STUMBLED and almost fell, but she managed somehow to steady herself, kept her feet and dashed on only to trip over a half buried rock a dozen feet ahead. She was breathless now and spent, and a fall was inevitable. However, she was able to cushion her fall somewhat by landing on her hands and knees. She forced herself up again presently, with a painful and dogged effort, and looked back furtively.

Her vision seemed a bit blurred at first, but it soon cleared. She could see the bridge in the distance, and the tall trees beyond it framed against the background of bright sky.

She suddenly realized that she was not being pursued, and the expression on her face was a reflection of her surprise. She felt easier then, and permitted herself to relax a little, only to jerk her head up again with startling suddenness when she heard a pounding of racing hoofs. The color—what little there was left—drained out of her face. She stared wide-eyed, fear mounting swiftly within her, but there was no one in sight, no one coming toward her from the direction of the bridge or the ranch itself. Then as her eyes shifted a gasp broke from her, for a horseman was coming whirling around the base of a steep, grassy slope. For a moment she was fear-rooted to the ground, incapable of movement, able only to see. She saw the man break into the open, saw him swerve his horse toward her. Now he was flashing over the ground at a breakneck pace. She managed to drag herself away and broke into a frantic run.

"Hey! Wait up!"

She heard his cry, but there was nothing familiar about it, and it served only to add to her terror and to goad her on. She was badly frightened, and therefore too confused to note that he was not the man who had accosted her.

The pounding of hoofs somewhere behind her swelled to a furious clatter. A sob burst from her. It was a prelude to hysteria—and capture.

She became aware of a strange and aching heaviness in her legs, noticed too a painful throbbing in her head. She found herself wincing, unconsciously of course, and it surprised her, because she hadn't realized before that her head ached. Her throat was parched—she hadn't noticed that before either. She tried to swallow and found herself gulping painfully and almost gagged. Her tongue seemed to have grown too large for her mouth. Then, to top it all off, her lungs seemed about to burst.

She stumbled again, drunkenly, and plodded on blindly. She tottered, another and louder sob died in her throat, and she put out her hands as though she were groping for something to lean on. Her legs buckled under her and she crumpled up. . . .

She knew somehow, intuitively perhaps, that she had fainted, but she never knew how long it was before she regained consciousness. When she did come to it was sudden, and her first feeling was one of lightheadedness. She swallowed and winced with anticipation; she was surprised to find that the wince was unnecessary, since there was no pain. She couldn't understand that, couldn't understand how her parched throat had suddenly become moistened again.

She moved a bit and knew at once that she was on the ground, for her hands touched grass and she recognized it. Her head throbbed again and she sank back. It was comforting to lie back, to have something to rest against. Then a strange thought came to her—there was something odd about the tree she was resting against. It had arms, arms that held her gently but securely and made certain that she would not topple to either side. She sighed deeply. Suddenly she realized that it wasn't a tree at all; it was a man, and she was resting against his shoulder. Instinctively she tried to pull away from him, but a strong arm halted her.

"Mebbe yuh better stay put f'r 'nother minute," she heard a voice say.

She did not dispute the matter. The throbbing in her head had eased up considerably, but now a curious and annoying buzzing in her ears made its presence known, and she was quite content to rest until this too subsided. As yet she had not opened her eyes. She'd been almost afraid to. She'd open them presently, she told herself, when she felt equal to getting

38

up. Perhaps after a few minutes the buzzing would be gone. She sat back very still.

"How 'bout it?" the voice behind her asked presently. "Yuh feel awright now?"

She opened her eyes. The buzzing had ceased.

"Yes," she said after a moment's consideration.

The man moved. He bent over her suddenly, slid two big hands under her arms and lifted her lightly to her feet.

"There y'are."

"Thank you," she said. She raised her head and looked up at him. "Oh—it's you!"

Marshall, hands on hips, grinned down at her.

"Uh-huh," he said lightly. There was a canteen slung over his shoulder. He suddenly remembered it and swung it around and held it out to her. "Want s'more water?"

"No, thank you. I've had enough."

"Whatever yuh say," he said with a shrug. The canteen thumped against his side. "Why'd yuh keep on runnin' f'r? Didn't yuh hear me holler to yuh?"

"Yes, that's why I ran."

He grinned again, boyishly.

"Oh, scared yuh, huh?"

She nodded in reply.

"Yes, almost as much as that man did when he fired at me," she answered.

"He didn't fire at yuh—that was me blastin' away at him," Marshall explained.

Her eyes widened with surprise.

"You?"

"Uh-huh. He was gettin' set t' rope yuh when I plugged him."

"Oh!"

"Mind tellin' a feller what that bus'ness was all about?" he asked, nodding in the general direction of the bridge. "I was up 'bove yuh, on th' rise 'bove the bridge. I could see what was goin' on down b'low me, but I couldn't hear nuthin', an' it had me kinda puzzled. Who was that feller?"

"I don't know. I never saw him before."

"That a fact?" He seemed surprised. "Then yuh don't even know what he was doin' there, or what he wanted of yuh?"

She shook her head.

"No, I don't. However, I think he was posted there purposely—probably to intercept me. You see, I did get a glimpse—it really wasn't much more than that—inside the ranch. There were several men sprawled out there, on the ground, you know, and they looked like they were—"

He eyed her sharply now.

"Dead?"

She nodded again, soberly.

"H'm. Who owns that place?" he asked, turning.

She followed his eyes.

"That's the Halliday ranch," she replied. "The Bar JH."

She saw his eyebrows arch.

"Oh, yeah?" He studied the distant Bar JH more interestedly now. "So that's th' Halliday place. What d'yuh know!"

"What do you mean?"

"Huh? Oh, nuthin'. Reckon I was just thinkin' out loud," he said quickly. He turned to her again. "An' you—you Halliday's daughter?"

"Well, not really," she answered.

"I don't savvy that."

"Jim Halliday raised me, gave me his name," she explained; "however, that's the only claim I have to actually being a Halliday."

"Oh."

"You see," she went on quickly, "I never knew anything about my parents, never even knew their names. I lost them when I was very young. Daddy Jim found me and tried to question me, but it seems the only thing I could say was something that sounded to him like 'June.' He decided that that was my name. I don't know—perhaps it is my name. Anyway, everyone's called me June ever since, and the Halliday part—well, you might say I came by it quite naturally."

"Uh-huh. What d'yuh s'ppose happened back there b'fore you come ridin' along?" he asked.

"I don't know for certain; however, I have an idea."

"Awright—what is it?"

"Raiders," she said simply.

"Uh-huh. You folks been bothered by 'em b'fore?"

"I don't mean the usual kind of raiders," she explained. "Daddy Jim had some trouble with a man named Barnes—Jess Barnes."

40

"Jess what? Barnes? What's this feller look like?"

"Oh, he's tall and wiry and mean-looking. His brother Sam is the Sheriff."

"Uh-huh. Reckon that's th' same polecat, awright."

"You've met him?"

"Yeah—yuh might put it that way. But what about this here trouble yuh were talkin' 'bout?"

"Well, Jess Barnes kept after Daddy Jim, trying in every way possible to induce him to sell the Bar JH. Of course Daddy Jim refused to consider such a thing. Barnes got nasty, even threatened us. Daddy Jim ordered him off the place and told him to stay off."

"An' Barnes took that?"

"No, he didn't. He swore he'd fix us and that he'd get the place in spite of us," she concluded.

"What'd Halliday do 'bout 'im?"

"Not very much. You see, he's dead."

Marshall nodded grimly.

"I know—they 'ccused me o' killin' 'im."

Her eyes widened instantly.

"You? Then—then you're the man the posse's been hunting?"

"Reckon so."

She seemed confused now, puzzled and for the moment frightened again. She probed his face.

"But you didn't—you couldn't have—"

He shook his head.

"Nope," he said.

She seemed relieved then.

"F'r my money, that Jess Barnes, if he didn't do th' killin' 'imself, shore knows who did do it," Marshall said. "It all points t' him havin' somethin' t' do with it. Figger it out f'r y'self an' see what it all adds up to."

She was looking up at him, listening to him attentively.

"T b'gin with," he went on, "Barnes wanted th' place, an' fr'm th' looks o' things he wanted it bad, too. What he wanted it f'r ain't important, although yuh c'n bet all yuh got that he wasn't after th' Bar JH so's he could go into ranchin'. That's hard work, ranchin' is, an' it don't allus foller that it's gonna pan out. B'sides, Barnes' kind go after big money, easy money an' quick money—see? Then, fr'm what yuh've told me 'bout

41

'im an' fr'm what I've seen of 'im, I'd say when he goes after somethin' he ain't a-tall p'rticular how he gets it."

He turned away and stared moodily over the range. He rubbed his chin thoughtfully with a big finger. Presently he turned to her again.

"He an' 'is brother, th' Sheriff—reckon they got things pretty well sewed up 'round here, ain't they?" he asked.

"Sewed up?" she repeated. "Oh, if you mean do they run things around here—why, yes, they do."

"Uh-huh, kinda figgered that."

"Sam," she added as an afterthought, "isn't a bad sort, criminally bad, I mean. It's merely that he's weak and that he does as he's told—as Jess tells him to do."

Marshall frowned.

"H'm. Then appealin' t' th' law f'r help'd be just a waste o' time an' effort, wouldn't it?"

June nodded.

"I'm afraid it would," she admitted.

He rubbed his chin again with his finger.

"Looks t' me like yuh're playin' 'gainst a stacked deck," he began. "Got 'ny friends 'round here—folks who'll stand up f'r yuh?"

"Yes. Daddy Jim was friendly with Charley Davis. Do you know him?"

"Nope, but that don't make 'ny diff'rence. Where's this Davis feller's place at?"

"South of here about twelve miles."

"Then th' best thing f'r you t' do is t' head f'r there pronto. Yuh're on'y a girl, y'know. You can't expect t' go after this Barnes feller by y'self. That's a man's job."

He turned abruptly and whistled. The black, idling a short distance away, looked up, whinnied and came trotting over. Marshall turned to the girl.

"Think yuh c'n show me how t' get t' th' Davis place fr'm here?" he asked.

"Of course," she said quickly.

Then she seemed suddenly thoughtful, hesitant over something.

"S'matter?"

"I was just thinking," she replied. "Charley Davis was a member of the posse that went after you. He told me so himself. Do you think it would be wise for you to go there with me?"

He considered the matter for a moment.

"Oh, I dunno," he said presently. "Still, I s'ppose th' smart thing'd be t' drop yuh off there, just about close enough f'r yuh t' be able t' reach th' place on foot. Mebbe it'd be better if Davis didn't know that I was aroun'."

He bent suddenly, swept her lightly off the ground and swung her up into the saddle. The black turned his head and looked up at her curiously. Marshall reached for the reins, caught them tightly and vaulted up behind the girl. He wheeled the black, jerked the reins sharply. The big horse loped away toward the south.

Charley Davis sat at the open window of his kitchen. There was an angry gleam in his eyes and tiny white patches danced in his bronzed cheeks. Charley's hair was grey and thin, and when he was angry or annoyed his hair seemed to bristle. A scowl darkened his face when he saw the slim, graceful, girlish figure of an aproned young woman come around the side of the house from the direction of the bunkhouse. He watched her through narrowed eyes, saw her turn and look back and wave her hand; then she came up the narrow gravel path that led to the kitchen door. Charley shifted himself in his chair, turned and faced the door. In another minute she would be coming in and—

"Why, Charley! I didn't expect you back so soon!"

Davis' lips thinned into a straight line.

"I c'n see that," he said coldly, controlling his mounting anger. "Been down t' th' bunkhouse, again, eh? Soon's I'm outta sight, yuh make a beeline f'r it, don'tcha?"

"Now, Charley. . . ."

"Don't Charley me! Young Haley's in, eh?"

"For Heaven's sake, Charley, won't you ever—"

"No!" he thundered, and bounded to his feet. "Now lemme tell yuh somethin', Stella!"

The young woman straightened up. There was no fear in her. She faced him calmly, patiently, defiantly. There was a definite trace of scorn in a cold smile that suddenly appeared over her mouth.

"Yes?" she asked tauntingly.

"Stella, f'r th' last time, stay th' hell away fr'm th' bunk-house, understan'? If I ever ketch yuh goin' down there again, or if I ever ketch yuh even glancin' at Haley, by God, I'll—"

"You'll what?"

Davis' face was livid now.

"Stella," he said thickly. "I'm warnin' yuh—wife or no wife—I'll—"

A sharp knock on the door interrupted him. He snapped his jaws shut. Stella laughed softly, turned on her heel and flung open the door.

"June!" she said in surprise. She turned momentarily in the doorway. "Charley, it's June Halliday!"

Davis scowled darkly.

"June, honey!" he heard Stella say delightedly. "Come in!"

He shook his head, mumbled something under his breath and trudged forward to join his wife.

CHAPTER 7

IT WAS EVENING, and Angels' Cafe was crowded and noisy. The air was oppressively thick from tobacco smoke that hung like a billowing cloud over the place, while the strong, pungent smell of malt and ale and beer assailed one from the very moment one entered through the open doors. However, no one appeared to notice it, or mind it.

At a corner table, which afforded its occupants a fair degree of privacy, sat three men, Jess Barnes and two others—one of them a stocky, swarthy, thick-necked and broad-shouldered man with sharp, piercing eyes that seemed to smolder ominously, even without provocation; his companion tall and lean, with placid blue eyes set in a smooth-skinned, boyish face that was topped off by a head of blond hair. His lips belied the rest of his face. They were thin, wantonly cruel, merciless—the lips of a man who would kill just for the sheer joy of killing.

There was a half-emptied bottle of whiskey on the table within reach of all of them. An empty glass stood in front of each man. Jess leaned forward over the table, resting his arms on it, and toyed with his glass. The swarthy man watched him for a moment.

"But what d'yuh aim t' do with th' Halliday place, Jess?" he demanded presently, impatience in his tone. "Don't tell me yuh got a hankerin' t' settle down an' try yore hand at ranchin'?"

Barnes laughed softly. He put down the glass and looked up.

"You oughta know me better'n that, Pecos," he replied.

The swarthy man shrugged his shoulder.

"Allus figgered I knowed yuh a heap better'n anyb'dy else did," he said calmly. "Now yuh got me wonderin'."

The blond man nodded.

"Like Pecos, reckon I've been doin' more'n my share o' wonderin', too," he drawled. "What's b'hind this grabbin' off o' Halliday's place?"

Jess smiled patiently. He looked from one to the other and finally shook his head.

"Dumber'n all hell, ain'tcha?" he chided. "Can't see past th' tip o' yore noses, c'n yuh—either o' yuh?"

Pecos scowled darkly. His companion flushed uncomfortably.

"When are you fellers gonna learn that when I do some-thin'—"

"Like killin' off Halliday?" Pecos asked innocently.

Barnes' eyes blazed.

"Watch yore tongue!" he snapped through suddenly thinned lips.

He swung around a bit in his chair and eyed the occupants of nearby tables; when he felt satisfied that Pecos hadn't been overheard, he turned around again, and looked hard at the swarthy man. Pecos glared back at him, but his eyes faltered presently and fell beneath Jess' steely gaze.

"Like I started t' say b'fore," Barnes began again in a calmer and colder tone, "you fellers oughta know by now that b'fore I make a play I gener'ly got somethin' doped out."

There was no comment from Pecos. The blond man nodded again.

"Yeah, reckon that's so, Jess. Wa-al, whatcha got planned now?" he asked. "Somethin' big an' worthwhile?"

Barnes permitted himself the luxury of a smile. However, it was not a pleasant smile; it was cold, scornful and derisive. He sank back in his chair.

"Big?" he echoed. "What d'yuh think I go after—chicken

feed?" He sat up again and leaned over the table. "Get closer an' pay some attention t' what I gotta say. I'm gonna let yuh in on somethin' that nob'dy knows—nob'dy but me."

His companions drew their chairs closer and leaned forward over the table too. Barnes glanced around him quickly, cautiously, before he went on; satisfied that no one could overhear him, he turned around again. He pushed the bottle aside, moved his glass out of his way, too.

"This," he began, drawing a circle on the table with his fingernail, "is th' Bar JH. Everyb'dy thinks it's 'n island. Swell—let 'em go on thinkin' that, 'cause that fits in with what we're gonna do. F'r yore inf'rmation, th' Bar JH ain't no island a-tall. Actu'lly it's nuthin' more'n tableland outta which th' mountains rise up—" he added the mountains to the circle he had drawn previously—"part on this side o' th' river, part on th' other side. Get it?"

Pecos grunted.

"Shore, so far."

"Awright then. Now, th' river b'gins underground—under th' mountains, understand?—'stead o' runnin' through th' mountains like folks think. Wa-al, s'ppose yuh hadda drive a herd o' steers across th' river, what would yuh do—take 'em across in rafts or somethin'? If yuh tried it, neither you nor th' steers'd live t' see th' other side, 'cause that current's so mean an' ornery that nuthin' could live in it. Now here's th' surprise. There's a hidden trail that nob'dy knows about—I'm willin' t' bet anythin' yuh like that Jim Halliday didn't even know 'bout it bein' there—an' this trail b'gins underground, back o' th' Bar JH, in th' foothills, an' if yuh foller it all th' way, yuh wind up on th' other side o' Thunder River. What d'yuh think o' that?"

Pecos' eyes widened.

"I'll be doggoned!"

Barnes' lip curled.

"Kinda figgered yuh would," he said dryly. "Now, what we're gonna do is work th' Bar JH like we were really ranchin'. 'Course it'll on'y be 'n act so's nob'dy'll ever get wise t' what's really goin' on there. What we'll actu'lly be doin' b'hind th' scenes is this—we'll run off every last head o' cattle we c'n reach, drive 'em across th' Bar JH, over that hidden trail I told yuh 'bout, an' take 'em across th' river. Once we've got

46

'em over there—hell, all we'll hafta do then is d'liver 'em an' collect f'r 'em an' come back. We'll have all th' 'rrangements t' dispose o' them made long b'fore we start over. So what we'll be doin' 'll be runnin' a kind o' clearin' house f'r cattle. See?"

There was a half-smile on Pecos' dark face; he was already visualizing the plan in operation.

"An' how!" he said enthusiastically. "Boy, an' I c'n see a heap more'n just that, too! Hell—'less we bungle it, we oughta be able t'milk every ranch' round these parts plumb dry of its cattle an' sell every danged head at a fancy price, 'cause they're scarcer'n all hell on th' other side o' th' river!"

Barnes looked at the blond man.

"Wa'al, Arizona?" he demanded. "What d'yuh think o' that set-up? Sound t' yuh like it might have possibilities f'r a clean-up?"

Arizona grinned boyishly.

"Yeah, it might," he acknowledged, and laughed.

"Thanks," Barnes said, and shoved the bottle closer to his companions. "Go 'head—fill 'em up."

The bottle was passed from one to the other, the glasses were filled and raised in silence, a nod of understanding passed between the three men, the glasses were drained and put down again.

"Now," Barnes began again. "So's yuh'll know what's been done a'ready—I sent Mexican Joe an' seven o' th' boys out t' th' Bar JH early this mornin' with orders t' dispose o' th' men Halliday had on th' place. I ain't heard fr'm 'em yet, but I woulda if things hadda gone wrong. Like's not they're busy gettin' th' place ready t' r'ceive what we run off t'night."

Pecos nodded understandingly.

"We're gonna swoop down on th' Circle D—Charley Davis' place—first," Barnes went on. "That's th' job f'r t'night— midnight. Yuh oughta have 'bout a dozen men. C'n yuh take care of it?"

"Midnight, eh?" Pecos repeated. He was hesitant for a moment. "That don't leave me a heap o' time; still, if I get goin' pronto, I oughta be able t' manage things awright. Yeah, you c'n figger on me handlin' it."

"Good f'r you. Now get this—Davis has some three thousand head grazin 'along th' river. Accordin' t' what I've been told, he's on'y got 'bout six men ridin' herd. Cut off a couple o' hundred head an' drive 'em north, still follerin' th' river. I'm headin' f'r th' Bar JH. I'll pick up some o' th' boys Mexican Joe's got there an' ride south t' meet yuh. Sound awright to yuh?"

"Shore."

"How 'bout me, Jess?" Arizona asked.

"Mebbe you better string along with Pecos f'r t'night," Barnes replied.

"Whatever yuh say."

Jess reached for the whiskey bottle, filled his glass again and pushed the bottle across the table.

"Help y'selves, boys. One more drink; then yuh better get goin'."

CHAPTER 8

IT WAS A DARK night, which met with Marshall's complete approval. It was a perfect night for his purposes. He had waited patiently for night to fall to pursue his intended investigation of the island ranch and now, alone and on foot— he had tethered the big black horse quite a distance from his objective—he crept forward toward the bridge.

Slowly and cautiously he went on, freezing in his tracks whenever he thought he heard a strange sound or spotted a shadow that resembled a human form. When he decided that the sound was purely imaginary and the shadow dissolved, he went on again. He reached the bridge finally and made his way down the embankment beside it, and just in time too, for at that very moment a couple of horsemen rode out from behind the wall of trees that screened the ranch.

Silently he managed to reach a point directly beneath the bridge; then the horsemen came clattering over it.

"Hold on a minute," Marshall heard a man's voice say overhead.

The horses were promptly reined in, midway across the wooden span. For a moment Marshall was puzzled. There was no fear in his mind that he had been detected, yet he wondered why they had stopped, wondered about it until he heard hoof beats approaching from another direction, from the range behind him.

"Someb'dy comin', awright," another man said.

"No kiddin'," the first man said sarcastically. "I've been wonderin' whether them cup-handle ears o' yores were good f'r anythin' b'side stoppin' yore hat fr'm slidin' down over yore neck."

"Aw, Joe. . . ."

The clatter of galloping hoofs swelled.

"Whoa!" a voice cried; then: "That you there, Joe?"

"Yeah," the first man replied. "Come ahead, Barnes, on'y watch yore step. There's water on both sides o' this here bridge —cold water, too, an' deep."

Barnes? Marshall bristled to attention. This was better than he had hoped for.

"What brings yuh here t'night?" the man who had answered to the name of "Joe" asked as Barnes' horse clattered onto the bridge and halted again presently almost directly above the very spot where Marshall was crouching so attentively.

"We're makin' our first move t'night," Jess answered. "Pecos an' Arizona an' a bunch o' th' boys are pullin' off a raid on th' Circle D—Charley Davis' place."

"Oh, yeah?" There was surprise in Joe's voice. "Ain't wastin' 'ny time, are yuh?"

"Time's money," Barnes snapped. "I don't aim t' waste 'ny —one or th' other."

"S'awright with me, Jess," Joe said quickly. "Hell, I c'n savvy that th' sooner we actu'lly get things started, th' sooner we'll all be able t' get t' see some o' that big money yuh promised us."

" 'Course. Yuh all set up here?"

"Ready an' waitin'. What time d'yuh figger Pecos'll be showin' up?"

"Oh, he oughta reach th' Circle D somewheres 'round midnight," Barnes replied. "He oughta be comin' this way 'most any time after that, say 'bout 'n hour after."

"An it's on'y 'bout 'leven now. Heck, we got heaps o' time then b'fore we c'n even b'gin t' expect 'im."

"Uh-huh. Say—got 'ny grub 'round th' house?"

"Plenty," Joe answered.

"Then s'ppose yuh lead me to it? I'm plumb holler inside. Oh, yeah, Joe—I tol' Pecos some of us'd ride out t' meet 'im, y'know, case any o' Davis' hands try t' foller 'im. After we eat we c'n get started."

"Whatever yuh say. Awright—let's go back."

The horses were wheeled. Presently they were jogging over the bridge again, retracing their steps to the tree-walled ranch. Barnes clattered along at the rear of the party. In a minute they were gone. Marshall edged his way out from under the bridge, trudged up the embankment, turned once and looked back. There was no one on the other side of the bridge, or on the opposite embankment. He dashed away into the darkness.

Shadows bathed the darkened, sprawling Circle D ranch-house—shadows that were huge and fantastically like long black icicles. There was a grove of tall trees behind the house —tall, motionless trees that thrust themselves skyward and lost themselves in the upper reaches of the night light; tall trees with full, far-spreading, overhanging branches that draped a mantle of obscuring darkness over the sleeping house.

Marshall dismounted in the deep shadows between two trees that faced the house. He looked about him curiously, his keen eyes sweeping the place in an all-absorbing glance.

"They shore sleep th' sleep o' th' dead 'round here," he muttered, and started toward the house.

He froze in his tracks, rigid and tensed, when a window along the front of the darkened house was suddenly and quietly opened. The slim, skirted figure of a girl mounted the sill, slid over it and dropped lightly to the ground.

"H'm—" he muttered again. "What's this?"

The girl was motionless for a moment.

"Don't look like June fr'm here," he told himself presently. "Nope, June's lighter'n this girl an' mebbe a mite shorter, too. Wonder who she is, an' why she's hightailin' it through th' window 'stead o' usin' th' door?"

Now the girl moved. She bent low and crept along, hugging the shadowy wall of the house for safety. Presently she was clear of the house. She straightened up and darted away,

50

swerving away from the house, then, to Marshall's complete surprise, she came racing directly toward him. Hastily he retreated, backing deeper in the shadows. Then the girl swerved again, sharply this time, and headed for a tall cottonwood just beyond the spot where Marshall stood. He breathed a bit easier and quickly shifted his eyes. The tall figure of a man appeared and halted beneath the cottonwood.

"Uh-huh," Marshall grunted. "So that's it. Shoulda knowed there'd be a man somewheres aroun' t' bring a girl up outta bed at this hour o'night."

The girl dashed past him and skidded up to the waiting man.

"Tom!" she panted delightedly. "You did come! I'm so glad!"

"Wa-al, I wasn't gonna come," the man answered doggedly in guarded tones. His voice was surprisingly youthful—the voice of a boy of twenty. "Stella, we gotta cut it out, y'hear? I've come here t'night, f'r th' last time, t' tell yuh so. This can't go on. Davis is my boss an' he's allus done th' right thing by me. Doggone it, this is like stabbin' 'im in th' back. I'm so plumb ashamed o' m'self I don't dare look in th' lookin'-glass when I'm combin' m' hair. I'm low-down, I'm—"

"Tom!" She was straining against him now, her arms around his neck. "Tom!"

"Doggone it, Stella, ain't I just—"

She crushed her lips against his, and his protestations died in his throat. Slowly, almost reluctantly at first, his arms came up around her, encircling her. The warmth of her young, eager body, the passion in her kiss communicated themselves to him. His strong arms tightened around her. They clung to each other, locked in each other's arms. After a minute he reached up and unclasped her hands, drew them down over his chest and pushed her away.

"Reckon that'll be all, Stella," he said with finality. His voice trembled a bit. Unconsciously he wiped his mouth with the back of his hand.

"Tom!"

"Stella, f'r Pete's sake, cut it out, will yuh?"

She threw her arms around him again.

"I won't—and I won't let you go either!"

"Doggone it," he sputtered helplessly. "What'm I gonna do with yuh, Stella? How c'n I make yuh understan' things?"

Marshall began to back up again. He hadn't intended to

eavesdrop, certainly it hadn't been part of his plan to spy on them. He backed slowly and for the second time in the span of minutes jerked to an abrupt halt. From out of the darkness came another man. He appeared so suddenly, so completely out of thin air that Marshall stared at him in amazement. However, he gave no indication that he had seen Marshall—his eyes were fixed upon the two young people beneath the cottonwood.

"Stella!"

The girl whirled like a cat, shielding the youth with her body. Moonlight broke through the dark sky and gleamed on the barrel of a leveled gun in the newcomer's hand.

"Step away fr'm 'im!" he commanded.

"Charley, please—wait!"

"Do's I say, y' hear? Step back fr'm 'im!"

"No!"

The muzzle of the gun came up just a bit.

"Awright—reckon it's more yore fault 'n it is his anyway, you—"

A sudden roar of gunfire from somewhere beyond them drowned him out. In the distance, from the direction of the river, the flashes of flaming guns stabbed the night sky. Charley wheeled and stared hard for a moment; there was no movement on the part of either of the others. He faced them again presently.

"Reckon you an' him'll hafta wait. I'll 'tend t' yuh both later on."

He wheeled and dashed toward the house. Stella raced after him; the youth in turn started after her.

"Stella!" he cried. "Wait—wait up!"

A trio of horsemen came thundering up out of the night. Afterwards, in an effort to piece things together again, Marshall decided that they too had come from the direction of the river, despite the fact that he hadn't heard the clatter of their horses' hoof beats until they were almost upon him. He reasoned that in all likelihood they had crept up in an encircling movement to avoid detection, reached a hidden point close to the house itself, then burst out in an effort to complete their surprise attack.

Tom skidded to a halt midway between the house and the cottonwood—Charley, with Stella racing at his heels, had already disappeared behind the house—and stared at the on-rushing horsemen in evident surprise. When he whirled and plunged on again, instead of hailing the newcomers or giving some outward sign of recognition, Marshall realized that they weren't Circle D riders as he had supposed. He sensed in that moment that they were raiders, members of Barnes' gang. His guns leaped into his hands. However, the horsemen failed to spot him; it was the youthful, fleeing Tom alone whom they beheld.

Flame burst from the gun of one of the raiders. Tom stumbled awkwardly and came to a faltering, painful halt. He turned toward the mounted men, his right hand streaking for his holster. It came away presently, empty. He sagged suddenly and pitched forward on his face.

Marshall's guns roared spitefully, gunfire that burst with the ear-splitting and startling suddenness of summer thunder. The man whose gun had felled Tom tumbled out of his saddle. His two companions, evidently suspecting that the surprise attack had backfired, whirled their horses around, dug their spurs into them and sent them bounding away. Marshall dashed out. His guns boomed a second time. A horse cried out, stumbled and fell, and his rider shot out of the saddle and plunged forward over his mount's head. He rolled away, escaping somehow the threshing hoofs of his screaming horse, scrambled to his feet, gun in hand, narrowly avoided being run down by an oncoming mate's horse and raised his gun.

Marshall and he fired as one. The twin Colts spoke with far greater accuracy and overwhelming authority. The leaden blast hurled the man backward and sent him crashing to the ground, a scant six feet beyond his fallen horse. The third man disappeared in the darkness.

Marshall holstered his guns, dashed over to where the youthful Tom lay sprawled, and turned him over on his back.

"Yuh hit bad?" he asked.

There was no reply, no sign of life from the youth. Marshall shook his head.

"Pore kid," he muttered. "He never had a chance."

He suddenly remembered that the youth had reached for his gun—remembered too that Tom's hand had come away from his holster empty. He bent down, reached the holster and frowned. It was empty. Marshall puzzled over it for a moment. A puncher without his gun was unheard of; besides—a muffled shot came from the direction of the house. He looked up quickly, and had started toward the house when he heard a door slam somewhere in the darkness near the corral. He halted and looked back. Men came running from the direction of the bunkhouse. Marshall dashed on, swung around the house, swerved sharply when an idling horse loomed up directly in his path and skidded to an abrupt stop. He stared hard with widening eyes at what he saw.

On the ground, not more than a dozen feet away, lay a sprawled motionless figure, face downward in the grass. Kneeling beside it and moaning loudly was the girl, Stella. Swiftly yet stealthily Marshall slipped past her, reached a clump of brush and stepped behind it just as a handful of men burst around the house and came lumbering up.

"Help!" the girl screamed. "Somebody—please!"

The men rushed up to her and crowded around.

"What in blazes—" a man began.

"Those men!" Stella screamed hysterically. "They killed him!"

Two or three of the men bent over the prone rancher and turned him over on his back.

"Charley, ain't it?" a man asked.

"Who d'yuh think it is, yuh dumb wit," another snapped.

"Yep," a third voice suddenly grown hard said heavily. "It's Charley, awright, an' he's dead—dead's he'll ever be."

The clatter of approaching horses' hoofs caused one of the men to straighten up. He dashed away, and returned a minute later followed by two horsemen who dismounted without delay and strode forward.

"Sorry t' hear 'bout Charley," the first rider began. "He was a square shooter, awright, 'bout th' best boss I ever had."

"Yeah," another man said. "Charley on'y knowed one way t' play, an' that was th' fair way. Too bad he hadda die without gettin' a chance t' hit back at them raiders. How'd you fellers down at th' river make out?"

"Not so good. They shore raised plenty o' hell with us. They plugged Baldy an' that Curly Morris, th' new hand, y'know, an' run off mebbe three hundred head b'sides scarin' holy hell outta th' rest o' th' herd. Oh, excuse me, Stella—reckon I f'rgot t' notice that that was you a-kneelin' there."

"Who's that layin' out in front o' th' house?" the second rider asked.

"Dunno," one of the others replied. "Whoever he is, he'll hafta stay put f'r now, leastways till we get 'round to 'im. Right now we got things t' do. Couple o' you fellers tote Charley inside. C'm'on, Stella—I'm gonna take you in first."

Stella's sobbing burst out anew. She refused his proffered hand, refused to let him touch her, at first; but finally she subsided and permitted him to help her up. He led her into the house, turned in the doorway and looked back over his shoulder.

"Awright, you fellers," he called. "Come ahead."

The other men lifted the lifeless body of Charley Davis and carried him inside.

Marshall, half crouching behind the brush did not stir. His face was curiously hard and grim. In his mind he was reliving the events of the crowded past half-hour, reliving them in as orderly a series of sequences as possible so as to avoid all chance of error. Through his mind flashed a profusion of scenes, which he began to sort into their proper places. There was the youthful Tom, staggering, groping for his gun and finding his holster empty, finally pitching forward on his face; there was the sprawled body of his employer, face downward in the grass, dead as the result of a bullet fired after the lone surviving raider had fled.

In his ears rang the youth's cry:

"Stella! Wait—wait up!"

Why had he cried out to her—why had he sought to stop her? The answer was all too obvious. The evidence was circumstantial, but it was conclusive and damning.

Stella had evidently yanked the gun out of the boy's holster; suspecting Stella's purpose, Tom had tried to stop her. A raider's bullet had interrupted him, stilled his voice forever. In his moment of agony, with a bullet in his vitals, he had forgotten that his holster was empty, hence his attempt to reach for his gun, a purely mechanical and unconscious movement on his part to fight back.

There was no doubt now in Marshall's mind—Stella had killed both men, one indirectly, the other directly. Marshall crouched a bit lower as the back door opened and two men emerged.

55

"Shore tough on Stella," Marshall heard one man say.

"An' how," his companion added.

They shook their heads and trudged away.

CHAPTER 9

WHEN THE LAST of the Circle D punchers had finally left the ranchhouse and plodded off toward the bunkhouse, Marshall emerged from his hiding place.

He listened for a moment, waiting until the last retreating footfall had faded out. He heard a door slam somewhere beyond him—decided that it was the bunkhouse door that had been slammed—heard the braying of a mule from the direction of the corral and, immediately after, the more distant whinny of a horse. He started forward. The grass was thick and lush and it cushioned his footsteps. He glanced at the back door of the house as he came abreast of it, trudged past it and started around the house, reconsidered almost immediately and backed into the shadows and peered out. There was no one about. Silence had settled over the Circle D again—this time a gentle, more natural silence, not a forbidding stillness as before. He noticed too that it was lighter, and he looked skyward. The moon had cast off its unfamiliar cloak of shyness, and now the vast sky was silvery bright.

He made his way along the side of the house, keeping close to the shadowy wall just as Stella had done half an hour before. He jerked to an abrupt halt when he thought he heard an approaching footstep, and stiffened for a moment, waiting expectantly, but no one appeared and the sound died away. Once, too, a shadow just ahead of him suddenly rose up, like a man straightening himself up to his full height, and Marshall backed swiftly against the wall, his hands tightening instinctively around his gun butts. But the shadow proved to be only a shadow and it soon dissolved. Marshall grunted inwardly and went on again, only to pull back hastily when he came abreast of a lighted window.

At that moment the blind was pulled down over the window.

Fortunately it was half an inch short of the sill, and a tiny ray of light sifted through the gap and over the sill and cast a yellowish gleam over the ground outside. Marshall crouched down, edged his way forward to the window and peered in.

It was a bedroom, evidently Stella's room, for there on the bed, in the very middle of the room, sobbing broken-heartedly, was Stella. There was someone with her, a golden-haired June who sat on the edge of the bed and leaned over Stella and smoothed her hair back gently and talked to her in an effort to comfort and console her; a gentle-voiced June who was clad in a heavy coat that was inches short of her ankle-length night-dress. Stella stopped crying for a moment, long enough for her to raise her head and edge her way closer to June and put her head in the younger girl's lap.

"There!" Marshall heard June say. "That's better, isn't it? Now please don't cry any more. You'll only make yourself ill."

If Stella answered in any way, Marshall did not hear her.

"To think that I slept through it all!" June said presently. "Now that I recall it, I'm sure I heard shots—oh, I know I did—but I must have imagined that they were just part of a terrible dream I'd been having and I probably drew the covers over my head and slept on."

Stella raised her head now and smiled wanly.

"It doesn't matter," she said. "You couldn't have done anything, you know."

"I suppose not."

Stella swung her legs over the side of the bed.

"I think you'd better go back to bed now, June," she said.

June's eyes widened.

"And leave you alone?" she asked incredulously.

Stella nodded.

"Please. I'd rather be alone now, if you don't mind. It's just—we-ll, it's just that I want to sit and think. You understand, don't you?"

"Yes, I suppose so. But you'll call me if you want me, won't you?"

"Of course."

"Well, all right then."

June arose slowly, turned and walked to the door. She opened it and looked back over her shoulder.

"I'll be awake," she said.

She went out, closing the door behind her. For a minute Stella was motionless; then she got to her feet. After listening intently, she marched swiftly to the door and locked it. She glanced at the window, a mechanical glance, unbuttoned the waist of her dress and drew out a gun. Marshall's eyes gleamed.

"Uh-huh," he muttered to himself. "There it is, awright, just as I figgered. That's th' boy Tom's gun, an' I'm willin' t' bet it's th' same gun that killed Davis."

There was a bureau against the far wall of the room. Stella turned toward it, checked herself and turned again, and retraced her steps to the bed. She placed the gun on the pillow, bent and pulled back the sheet and drew back one corner of the mattress, exposing the wire spring. Carefully she laid the gun on the spring, lowered the mattress, replaced the sheet, tucking it under the mattress tightly, and stepped back.

Marshall heard a heavy step near the front of the house and crouched low against the wall. He backed slowly toward the rear, crowding against the wall as closely as he could, then halted when the figures of two men came into view from the direction of the bunkhouse. They stopped presently and bent over something that lay in the grass in front of the house.

"Uh-huh," Marshall muttered to himself. "Musta just r'membered that there was someb'dy layin' out there."

"Hey, Mac!" a man yelled, either from the doorway of the bunkhouse or from its single window. "Doggone it, why'n hell can't yuh wait till mornin' b'fore yuh go fussin' over that polecat? He'll still be there then. Don't look t' me like he's plannin' t' go 'nywheres."

There was no reply.

"Who is it?" another voice called. "Reco'nize 'im, Mac?"

One of the men who was bending over the body of the youthful Tom—it was probably the man who had been addressed as "Mac"—straightened up and turned toward the bunkhouse.

"Reco'nize 'im?" he echoed. "'Course I do, dang it! It's th' Haley kid, an' he's dead!"

The door of the bunkhouse banged loudly. Evidently the men who had refused to bother with a dead raider were piling out again. Marshall could hear them coming, their boots thumping on the ground as they raced forward to where Mac and

58

his companion were standing. Marshall straightened up. Casting aside all caution, he plunged forward again toward Stella's window. He was certain that she had heard Mac's cry. He skidded up to the window, anxious to see Stella's reaction to the announcement, and peered into the room. A single look at her told him that she had heard it; her reaction to Mac's shouted discovery of the youth's dead body was unconcealed.

Stella had halted midway between the window and the bed. She was white-faced and wide-eyed and stiffly erect as though she had been shocked into rigidity. Her lips twitched fleetingly; then they moved.

"No!" she whispered. "It—it can't be!"

She stifled a scream with the back of a clenched fist. A great sob shook her. Slowly her head came down. Her arms fell limply. She turned brokenly, suddenly bent and tottering, and stumbled blindly toward the bed. She groped for it, reached it finally and crumpled up on it.

Marshall frowned and turned away from the window.

The long night had almost gone.

Slowly Marshall rode around the ranch until he found himself atop a rise that looked down upon the ranchhouse. Beyond it was the bunkhouse and the corral with its gleaming white bars. There he halted, dismounted and squatted down in the grass. The black idled a dozen feet behind him, nibbling with little appetite on a patch of fresh, young grass. From time to time the big horse looked up, but when Marshall made no attempt to rise, the black resumed his nibbling. He whinnied once, softly, and waited, but there was no response. The big horse made no further attempt to attract his master's attention or remind him of his presence.

A single yellowish light—it had probably burned throughout the night—gleamed with a wearied flickering in the uncovered window of the bunkhouse. The light seemed to hold Marshall's eyes; he shifted them away time and again, but always they returned to it.

Then the sun burst into the sky and flooded the range with light and warmth. Lingering shadows fled almost instantly. The light in the bunkhouse window flickered feebly and went out. Marshall sat upright now. The bunkhouse door was flung open and men plodded out, halting in the early morning sunlight to stretch themselves. Mechanically each man glanced skyward and blinked. One or two of them rubbed their eyes. Mechanically too, each man hitched up his pants and shifted his holster a bit and gave his hat brim a downward jerk. The door slammed shut behind them. One man wheeled and glared at the offending door. Silently and heavily they trudged off toward a distant, hulking building—the barn. They disappeared within it; presently the rasping sound of sawing, then the louder clatter of plied hammers drifted out from the barn.

Minutes passed, ten, twenty, perhaps more. The sawing ceased completely; then the sound of hammering died out, too. The men emerged, two of them shouldering a crudely fashioned coffin. There was an echoing clatter of hoofs and the creaking rumble of wheels, and a man drove a farm wagon up to the bunkhouse door. He braked the wagon and relaxed on the wide seat and waited. The coffin was carried inside; minutes later it was carried out again, this time on the shoulders of four of the men, who lifted it with an effort onto the wagon. One of the men climbed up beside the driver. The wagon rolled away again, the other punchers following behind it on foot. As they passed the corral, the mules poked their heads through the smooth-worn bars and eyed the cortege curiously, but none of them brayed.

Tom Haley's burial was a brief affair. The punchers who laid him to rest returned shortly, all of them riding in the wagon which pulled up in front of the barn. Two of the men jumped down, tramped into the building, and reappeared almost directly, carrying a second coffin. The box was lifted onto the wagon, the two men climbed up again and the wagon rumbled away. It clattered past the corral and the bunkhouse and came to a full stop directly in front of the ranchhouse.

All of the punchers, all of them save the driver, got down and marched up to the door which opened from within just as they reached it. There was a moment's conversation in the doorway; then two men again turned and retraced their steps to the wagon, removed the coffin and carried it into the house.

It was fully fifteen minutes before the body of Charley Davis was brought out and placed on the wagon. It was probably five minutes more before two women, Stella and June, emerged from the house. Stella halted abruptly and stared at the wagon and covered her face with her hands. June put her arm around her and held her close for a moment, whispering to her; then Stella straightened up again. June nodded to the driver. Another puncher stepped past them, climbed up on the wagon and slid into the seat beside the driver. The wagon started away. Stella and June marched after it, with the punchers falling in behind them.

For a second time the wagon led the way past the corral, and again the mules clattered up to the bars, thrust their heads through and looked out. This time a single mule brayed, wheeled and trotted away. The other mules wheeled too, slowly, and jogged off. The funeral party disappeared behind the barn.

Marshall climbed to his feet, hitched up his pants, glanced at the black and strode briskly past him, quickened his pace and broke into a run. For a moment the big horse seemed tempted to run after him, but Marshall turned and looked back at him and shook his head, and the black relaxed. Marshall raced down the incline, swerving sharply toward the rear of the ranchhouse. He came panting up to the kitchen door. It was unlocked and yielded to a single twist of his wrist. He stepped inside, closed the door quietly behind him and strode swiftly through the house until he came to a room which he recognized. It was Stella's room, and there was the window through which he had watched her hide Haley's gun. The window blind had been raised a bit, and the window itself was open. He stepped over to it and listened a moment. He could hear the milling mules in the corral, but there was no sound of the returning mourners. He turned on his heel and strode to the bed, threw back the covers and raised the corner of the mattress.

The gun was still there, just as Stella had placed it. Quickly, expertly, he caught it up. There was an air of confident anticipation about him and about his every movement; he was evidently definitely certain that the gun and what it would reveal would complete the cycle of evidence-finding. His eyes widened in surprise; in a twinkling they had narrowed. A deepening frown spread over his face. The gun was loaded, fully loaded, too.

For the moment he refused to allow it to disturb him. The fact that the gun was fully loaded meant little. It was a comparatively simple matter to insert a fresh cartridge in place of one that had been discharged.

He lifted the gun, brought it up to his nose and sniffed hard, first the muzzle, then the chamber.

Now he was both annoyed and puzzled, not so much by the disturbing fact that there was absolutely no odor of burnt gunpowder about the gun as he was by its implication. He sniffed hard again, shook his head finally and lowered the gun. He shifted it about in his hand idly. The letters "T. H." neatly burned into the wooden butt stared up at him. There was little doubt about the ownership of the gun. It was Haley's all right. . . .

Slowly he replaced the gun. Carefully he lowered the mattress. Carefully, too, he tucked in the sheet and the bedclothes, just as he had seen Stella do it. The puzzled look was still visible on his face as he straightened up and stepped back a bit to view his attempt at bedmaking. He smoothed down the blanket, patted it gently into evenness and turned away.

"I don't savvy it nohow," he muttered to himself. "I'da been willin' t' bet m' shirt on it that that was th' gun that blasted Davis t' death an' that it was th' girl, Stella, who done th' blastin'. But, hell—that gun proves I'm dead wrong on both counts. Th' danged thing ain't been fired in hell knows how long! Far's I c'n see, I'm just 'bout a hun'erd p'rcent worse off'n I was b'fore. Had a doggoned good, A-1 suspect then. Now all I've got is a dead man, but th' gun an' th' killer just ain't!"

CHAPTER 10

THE MUFFLED, grass-cushioned beat of galloping hoofs broke the crisp stillness of the early morning. A horseman, southward bound, came riding over the horizon, then downward along the grassy surface of a gentle slope and upward again until he topped a slight rise. The rider was swarthy and stocky, the man called Pecos. Now he swerved a bit more southerly, and reached behind him to jerk on a lead rope that ran from his saddle horn to a horse that clattered along behind him, June Halliday's golden mare, Honey.

The sun was bright now, a warm, cheerful sun that made Pecos feel better than ever before. Then he suddenly recalled how angry he had been just a few hours before. His face grew hard and grim—perhaps it got darker, too, as it usually did when his temper flared up. He was reliving his arrival at the Bar JH. The very thought of it made him angry again, almost as angry as he had been then.

He was pulling up in front of the Bar JH ranchhouse. He was dirty and unkempt, but he was so eager and excited that he forgot his weariness. Jess Barnes was waiting for him on the wide porch; now Jess was coming down the steps to meet him, halting finally on the bottom step. Pecos recalled that he had dismounted but that he had had to pull back hastily and crowd against his horse to avoid being trampled by the oncoming steers which he and the other men had "cut off" from the Circle D herd. The rustled steers were being driven toward the corral which had been made ready for them. In the morning they would be hustled out again and driven over the hidden trail that wound through the mountains and then onto the opposite side of the river.

There was a momentary lull in the proceedings. For some unknown reason a handful of steers suddenly halted, wheeled just as suddenly, lowered their heads and piled into their on-rushing mates. For a brief but almost eternally long minute there was confusion, until alert horsemen bore down upon the rebels and drove them back into line. Pecos took advantage of the situation to dash across the intervening space to the porch steps. Under control again, the steers started forward a second time, loping along in their lumbering, ungainly stride.

"Got away with 'em awright, eh?" he heard Jess ask. "Have 'ny trouble?"

"No more'n we could handle. Didn't need th' boys yuh sent out t' meet us, either."

"Uh-huh."

"Where's th' girl, Jess?"

"Dunno where she is, Pecos."

"Huh? What d'yuh mean yuh dunno? C'mon, Jess—quit stallin' an' tell me where yuh got 'er."

"I ain't got 'er."

"What are yuh givin' me?"

"Think yuh c'n listen f'r a minute, so's I c'n tell yuh what happened to 'er?"

"I c'n listen awright, on'y yuh better make it good."

"I aim to, Pecos. Blackie Wallace was standin' guard just outside, on this side o' th' bridge. Th' girl come along, not suspectin' a thing. 'Stead o' lettin' 'er come on an' grabbin' 'er afterwards, Blackie, th' fool, made a beeline f'r 'er an' musta scared hell out of 'er."

"Th' damn fool!"

"'Course. Anyway, she put up a fight, slid offa her horse an' started t' run back over th' bridge."

"Go on."

"Wa-al, Blackie got sore an' yanked off his rope. He was gonna teach 'er a lesson. He raised his arm t' throw when someb'dy drilled 'im, who it was nob'dy c'n figger out. Blackie f'rgot all about th' girl then, managed t' wheel his horse, just about made th' house, then toppled outta th' saddle. Couple o' th' boys picked 'im up an' toted 'im inside. He managed t' tell me what I've just told you; then he cashed in."

"Wa-al, th' hell with Blackie. He got what was comin' to 'im. It's th' girl I'm thinkin' of."

"I'm shore sorry t' disappoint yuh, Pecos."

"Yeah, I'll bet yuh are."

"Suit y'self. I told yuh what happened, an' that's that. If yuh don't wanna b'lieve me, that's awright, too. On'y if th' girl means s' damn much, go look f'r 'er."

"Yeah—where?"

"Use y' head, man. There are four ways she coulda gone. West, an' that means inter th' river. North—that's here. So that cuts th' four down t' two—right? Th' town lays toward th' east, an' yuh c'n be damn shore she didn't head that way. On'y d'rection she coulda gone in is south."

"Why south?"

"Ol' man Halliday was kinda friendly with Charley Davis, an' his place is south o' here. Does that tell yuh what yuh wanna know, or do I hafta draw yuh s'm pictures?"

"Don't bother, Barnes. I ain't that dumb."

"'Course yuh ain't. Pecos, if I was you I'd say th' hell with 'er an' f'rget about 'er."

"Yeah, you would—on'y you ain't me. See yuh later, Barnes."

"Where yuh goin'?"

"Places. So long."

Pecos stalked off angrily. Then he noticed a horse tied to a sturdy tree that stood alone almost midway between the house and the entrance to the ranch. The tree was totally unimportant. If he had noticed it before he failed to remember it now. He did recall that he had noticed the tethered horse as he had galloped past on his way toward the house; however, he had been preoccupied with something far more intriguing than a mere horse and he had promptly forgotten about it. But now, as he came abreast of it again, something made him stop and look at it. There was no explaining his halting there, for he was in a surly mood and not the slightest bit interested in the horse.

There was a man standing near the horse. Pecos recognized him as one of Barnes' newly acquired followers. Thumbs hooked in his gun belt, his head cocked a bit sideways, he was studying the horse with an appraising if not critical eye. He straightened up finally and nodded approvingly. He felt Pecos' eyes on him, and he turned toward him and nodded.

"Hi," he said amiably. "That there's a heap o' horseflesh, ain't it?"

Pecos was in no mood for idle conversation. He was surprised when he heard himself answer:

"Oh, I dunno. She don't look like anythin' extra special t' me."

"She don't, hey? Shows what you know 'bout horses, Mister. F'r my dough she's a honey an' nuthin' else but."

"S'awright with me."

Pecos started off again.

"Hey," the man called after him. "I s'ppose th' girl who owns this mare ain't anythin' extra special either, huh?"

Pecos jerked to an abrupt halt. Girl? He whirled and came striding back.

"Girl?" he repeated. "What girl?"

"Don'tcha know? Why, th' Halliday kid of course. That's who!"

"Oh, yeah?"

"Yeah."

Pecos bolted away. He raced directly toward his waiting horse, vaulted into the saddle, wheeled and came clattering back. The man looked up at him curiously.

"Untie 'er," Pecos ordered briefly.

"Huh?"

"S'matter—yuh deef?"

"Nope. I just don't savvy it. What's th' idea of untyin' 'er?"

"Mister, anyb'dy ever tell yuh that yuh were too damned nosy?"

"Heck, pardner, yuh oughta know I didn't mean nuthin'. Reckon I was just curious, that's all."

"Wa-al, 'round these parts, when a feller gets too curious somethin' gener'lly happens to 'im. Try mindin' yore own bus'ness, Mister, an' nob'dy'll know yuh're around. Mebbe then nuthin' 'll happen to yuh. Savvy?"

Honey was untied without further discussion. The tethering line was passed up to Pecos, who looped the loose end carefully around his saddle horn. As an added precaution he dismounted, strode back to the mare and examined the noose around her neck. Satisfied that the slip-knot would hold, Pecos nodded and attempted to pat the mare's neck. She shied away from him hastily. Pecos grunted, trudged off and climbed up into the saddle again.

"Where yuh goin' with 'er, pardner?" the man asked casually.

"T' hell," Pecos snarled. "Wanna come along?"

"No, thanks," the man answered with annoying calm. "I kinda got m' heart set on th' other place. If they turn me down, I'll r'member yore invite an' hunt yuh up."

Pecos' hand tightened around his gun butt.

Then he just managed to check himself. Under ordinary conditions he would have answered the fellow with a withering blast of lead, but at the moment he had more important business awaiting his attention.

He made a mental note to look up the man when he had more time, spurred his mount and cantered away.

CHAPTER 11

THE FRONT DOOR creaked and opened, and June Halliday emerged from the house and into the bright warm sunshine.

She halted in the open doorway, a bit hesitant or perhaps undecided, considered for a moment and finally stepped outside. She remembered that she had left the door open, turned and closed it quietly, turned again, quickly this time, when she heard approaching hoof beats, and looked up. A horseman came loping along, eastward from the range and the river. Now the man drew abreast of the house. He glanced at it, caught sight of June and touched the brim of his hat gravely, rode on, cantered past the bunkhouse and swerved away toward the corral.

June's eyes followed him. There were some eight or ten punchers ranged along the side of the corral. They were silent and thoughtful and solemn-faced, and all of them appeared to be eyeing the house as though they were waiting for something. Two of them clambered up to the top rail of the corral and seated themselves, made themselves as comfortable as the rail permitted and, as a precaution against a too sudden descent, hooked their toes in the rail below them. The other men leaned back against the bars with an air that indicated that they were prepared to wait there indefinitely.

The newcomer nodded to some of the punchers, those who looked up when he sauntered up to them, said something to one man and pushed past him apparently without waiting for a reply, found room between two men and squatted down, his back against a rail post.

June sensed what the men were thinking about, understood what they were waiting for and sympathized with them. Their employer was dead and they were genuinely sorry. Their silence and deep thought she attributed to something else. The ranch was Stella's property now, to do with as she alone saw fit. Obviously, then, what she proposed to do with it was what they were worrying about. If she decided to retain it, well and good, for then their jobs would be safe; she would make no changes in personnel. But if she decided to dispose of the Circle D—well, that would make a vast difference. Usually the sale of a ranch meant much more than just a change in ownership. Often it meant a change in policy, in manner of operation, and all too often the new owner arrived on the scene firmly convinced that the ranch could be operated more economically. That meant a general "housecleaning" in which the old employees would be the first to feel the weight of the none too considerate hand of the new owner.

June shook her head. She was sorry for them. She turned slowly and strolled around the house. She glanced at Stella's window as she came abreast of it. Her glancing at it was mechanical and unconscious rather than deliberate, and she turned her head away quickly and continued on toward the rear. She had no desire to intrude upon Stella's privacy. Stella had gone directly to her room following their return to the house, and June was relieved. She felt unequal to the task of buoying up Stella's spirits when her own were so badly in need of bolstering. She was glad to be alone; for she was facing a problem that was far weightier than the punchers'.

As far as they were concerned, if the Circle D did pass into another's hands, if they did lose their jobs—well, they could get others. Good men were scarce, and the far-flung ranches were always on the lookout for experienced riders.

She, on the other hand, had never had to work, to shift for herself—everything she had needed or wanted had been provided, and provided easily and amply. It was different now, she told herself grimly. From now on she would have to take care of herself and provide for herself. She would have to work, she would have to earn her meals, her lodgings, whatever else she might need, too.

She stumbled and jerked to an abrupt halt. She suddenly realized that she was trudging up a steep incline. Already she had negotiated more than half the distance to the top. It seemed incredible, but it was so. She turned and looked down. She saw the Circle D in a hollow, with the range rising above it on all sides. She debated with herself whether to go on until she reached the level of the rangeland or retrace her steps. She finally shrugged her shoulders. It didn't matter much either way. She plodded on again, panted up to the very top of the incline and halted again to get her breath.

She heard the shrill, high-pitched whinny of a horse and started, looking up quickly, excitedly, sweeping the open range with eager eyes. She had recognized the whinny—she had heard it too often to have forgotten it so quickly. It was Honey's. She heard it again. A cry of gladness burst from her lips.

"Honey!"

She stumbled forward blindly. Her eyes were suddenly filled with tears; however, the mist lifted in another moment. A hundred feet away, near a wide spread of brush, stood the golden mare. Honey raised her head and whinnied again, in response to June's cry. June flew over the ground. She panted up to the mare and threw her arms around Honey's neck.

"Honey—you darling!"

Strong, rough hands suddenly gripped her arms and tore her away from the mare. Before she could understand what was happening to her, June was swept off the ground and lifted into the saddle of another horse. A man vaulted up behind her, and imprisoned her within the hollow of a burly, unyielding left arm. She struggled desperately, frantically, to free herself, but Pecos would not be denied. A frenzied scream broke from her.

"Help!"

Pecos' arm tightened around her until she was as thoroughly helpless as if she had been bound. Now they were moving. The horse trotted, then broke into a canter. She made a last effort to escape. A sudden, surprising surge of strength enabled her to ease Pecos' hold on her, and she was able to raise her head a bit. The horse halted abruptly. Fifty feet ahead of them was a motionless horseman, a man astride a big black horse.

"Marshall!" June screamed.

She felt her captor's arm tighten around her again. Once more she was imprisoned in a vise-like grip. Pecos shifted the reins to his left hand, leaving his right hand free. It dropped and curled around the butt of his gun.

They swung a bit westward, toward the river. Marshall swerved as they did, just as much but no more. They swung eastward again, and Marshall followed, unhurried and evidently waiting. It was obvious that Marshall would not commit himself until Pecos made a definite move. Pecos stiffened in the saddle. He jerked the reins sharply, and the horse whirled and darted off again toward the river, only to be jerked to a stiff-legged halt when Marshall's big horse fairly skimmed over the ground and cut them off. Now Pecos wheeled and cantered back toward the Circle D. June was barely able to twist around for a brief glance. Marshall was following them, maintaining the original distance between them.

Pecos spurred his mount. They clattered over the ground and thundered up to the wide spread of brush, to the very spot from which she had been snatched up but minutes before. Pecos dismounted and dragged her out of the saddle. He threw his left arm around her, lifted her off the ground and carried her swiftly toward the brush. She struck at him, but he paid no attention to the blow. Then he dropped her suddenly. She landed on her hands and knees and looked up. Pecos' gun flashed into his right hand. Her eyes shifted to his face. It was dark and cruel. His eyes burned into June's.

"Do's I say an' yuh'll be awright, understan'?" he snapped. "Stay down there an' don't move 'less I tell yuh to!"

She heard a swift racing of hoofs. Pecos' gun jerked upward. It thundered mightily, deafeningly, and two shots tore through the brush. But the hoof beats seemed to flash past them as though Marshall was circling the brush, swinging around from east to west in an effort to come up behind them. Again Pecos' gun roared. The bullet fairly screamed with defiance as it ploughed through the thick brush and snipped off bits of twig that stood unflinchingly in its path as cleanly as though it were a scythe. There was a moment's heavy silence and another moment's tense wait, then Pecos grunted and lowered his gun and turned slowly toward the river, an indication that he expected Marshall's attack to come from that direction. He set himself firmly, as a man does in preparing to ward off a headlong charge, stiffened into rigidity, crouched the barest bit and raised his gun again. June looked past him. Her eyes widened. She stared with bated breath.

She saw a tall figure—a man who moved as swiftly and as noiselessly as a mountain cat—emerge from the brush a dozen feet behind the tensed Pecos.

There was a sudden thunder of hoofs, and Marshall's big black whirled around the western edge of the brush. Pecos' gun seemed to jump upward in his hand. Marshall hurled himself at the man, who staggered under the impact. Pecos' gun roared, but his aim had been deflected. The bullet swirled skyward, harmlessly.

The two men went down in a furious, threshing, tangled heap; June heard a fist thud home, and the threshing ceased.

Marshall scrambled to his feet. He shifted something from his left to his right hand. June saw that it was a gun, Pecos' gun. Marshall drew back his right arm and hurled the gun far into the brush. Now he was looking at June. She met his eyes and smiled wanly.

"H-hello," she said.

He grinned at her boyishly.

"H'llo y'self," he answered. "Yuh awright?"

"Yes, I think so."

"Good enough," he said cheerfully. "S'ppose yuh stay put there f'r just another minute while I kinda finish up with this feller?"

He bent over Pecos and dragged him to his feet. June got a glimpse of Pecos' face—it was battered and one eye seemed unusually puffy. There was a cut just below the eye, and a tiny trickle of blood appeared on his high cheek bone. The swarthy man swayed on unsteady, buckling legs.

"Who are yuh?" Marshall demanded. "An' what d'yuh want 'round here?"

There was no reply. Pecos sagged against him, and Marshall shoved him away. Pecos seemed to totter, but it was overdone and Marshall, on the alert, quickly backed away. The swarthy man hurled himself at his taller opponent. Marshall, still backing, nimbly side-stepped, pivoted and swung with the full weight of his body behind his swing. His left fist fairly exploded in Pecos' face. There was a fearful crash. Pecos went over backwards. Marshall circled him warily, then, when he was apparently satisfied that the man was through, he relaxed, straightened up again, caught June's eye and grinned at her.

"Reckon that'll be 'bout all fr'm him," he said lightly.

He hitched up his belt and started toward her.

June smiled, and then, as Marshall came up to her, she quietly crumpled up.

CHAPTER 12

STELLA TURNED, caught Marshall's eye and nodded.

"She's coming to," she said in a low voice.

June stirred slightly. Stella arose from her chair beside the bed, tiptoed across the room to the window and raised the blind. There was a sudden, overwhelming rush of dazzling sunlight. Fleet, darting rays danced over the ceiling and walls, over the bed and over the slim figure outstretched upon it. June stirred a second time, sighed and opened her eyes. Quickly she raised her hand to shield her eyes from the light. Stella retraced her steps to the bed and bent over her.

"Well!" she said cheerily. "That's more like it!"

She smoothed back June's hair, recaptured a stray strand and tucked it back in place.

"Feel better?" she asked.

June's lips parted in a smile.

"Oh, yes," she answered. "Much better."

Her eyes shifted away from Stella to the foot of the bed, to Marshall, who was standing there quietly and motionlessly, looking down at her. Her eyes ranged over him—he was even bigger and broader of shoulder than she had realized. Suddenly too, and this gave her a pleasant and exciting jolt, she became aware of something else about him, something she had evidently failed to notice before—he was positively good-looking.

His eyes were clear and steady, his mouth fairly generous in size and his chin firm. That was a sign of character and strength, and she nodded approvingly. As for his nose, it was neither too pronounced nor too small, but just about the right kind and size. And then there was his hair. She wasn't particularly certain about the color, but she liked it, liked the way he wore it, liked the casual, boyish way a stray lock wandered off and curled above his right eyebrow. There was a certain charm about a boyish man that appealed to her; he had that particular charm. He would take a lot of aging before he finally looked old.

Their eyes met. June suddenly became aware of it and, properly feminine in her reaction, blushed and quickly looked away. Marshall hastily lowered his eyes.

"Now, young lady," Stella began again, "how would you like a cup of coffee?"

"U-m-m—I'd love it."

Stella looked over her shoulder at Marshall.

"You'll have a cup, too, won't you?" she asked.

Marshall considered, and finally shook his head.

"No, reckon not," he replied. "Thanks just th' same, Ma'am."

"Ma'am!" Stella bristled with indignation. "You must think I'm an old woman!" She turned again. "June, I give up. He's impossible. He simply won't accept a thing from me. Oh, the coffee isn't the only thing he's turned down. I offered him a job here, a foreman's job, mind you, and he turned that down too. I wish you'd see what you can do with him. Perhaps you can persuade him to accept."

Marshall grinned sheepishly.

"You're shore makin' me feel plumb ashamed o' m'self," he said.

Stella wheeled, her hands on her hips.

"Well?" she demanded tauntingly.

There was a definite challenge in her voice, in her eyes, in the way she looked at him. There was seductiveness, consciously there or otherwise, in the saucy way in which she tilted her shapely head. There was an easy grace, an almost deliberate air of abandon in her every movement. Marshall thought of Charley Davis and of Tom Haley—how weak and putty-like they must have been in her hands.

"Well?" he heard her ask again.

"Huh? Oh. Wa-al, first off, I ain't lookin' f'r work. Might even go so far's t' say that I'm avoidin' it."

"Indeed!"

"Uh-huh," he said calmly. He was being annoyingly calm; he wanted to show her that she hadn't overwhelmed him too. "Y'know, th' way I look at it, a job an' a sickness are pretty much alike. Th' longer yuh have 'em, th' more they grow on yuh. First thing yuh know, they've b'come part o' yuh. Finally,

73

there's no gettin' rid o' either one, 'cause tryin' t' shake 'em off is like tryin' t' cut off part o' yuh an' leavin' it b'hind. It can't be done."

"Go on," Stella commanded.

"I aim to. Now s'pposin' I take a job, say th' one you offered me. I'd prob'bly get t' like it so much I'd never have th' courage t' quit, even though I'd never be happy 'cause I'd allus have a hankerin' t' see California."

"California?" Stella repeated.

Marshall nodded.

"Uh-huh, that's where I'm headed f'r," he said simply.

Stella's face clouded.

"Oh," she said slowly. "I see. Well, that's unfortunate—for us, I mean. It was my intention to hold on to the ranch, provided, of course, that I could hire a good man to run it. It's too much for a woman—it needs a man, as you know. However, if I can't, I can't, and that will be that. I'll simply dispose of the place."

She marched briskly to the door, opened it, halted in the doorway and looked back over her shoulder.

"I'll be back directly with your coffee, June," she said.

The door closed behind her. There was a moment's silence, an awkward interlude during which June and Marshall each waited for the other to speak.

"That man—" June began, and looked up.

"Huh? Oh, one o' th' punchers here recognized 'im. He's one o' Barnes' outfit," Marshall replied. Then as an afterthought and in an attempt to allay her fears, he added, "Got 'im tied up in th' barn with a couple o' th' men standin' guard over 'im an' wishin' he'd make a break so they could fix 'im good. Anyway, you needn't worry 'bout him—he won't bother yuh again."

"All right, if you say so."

She lay back against her pillow for another moment, silent and evidently thinking.

"California," she mused. "It must be wonderful country."

"Yeah, so I've heard," Marshall added. "D'yuh mind if I change th' subject an' ask yuh somethin'? What's gonna b'come o' you if she—if Missus Davis sells th' place?"

June's eyes faltered and finally fell beneath his steady gaze.

"Oh, I'll be all right."

"Yeah, how?"

"Why—why, I'll simply get something to do."

"H'm—just like that, eh?"

The door opened and Stella returned, carrying a small tray. Steam curled lazily upward from a cup of coffee on the tray. She went directly to the bed.

"Missus Davis—" Marshall began.

June sat up, and Stella placed the tray in her lap.

"Yes?" Stella asked over her shoulder.

"That job yuh offered me b'fore—is it still open?"

Stella turned to him quickly.

"Of course."

"Awright then. I'm taking it."

"Stella," June said quickly, "he doesn't really want it. He's taking it because—"

"B'cause I want it," Marshall said, interrupting her. "Man c'n change his mind, can't he?"

Stella studied him for a moment.

"Yes, he can, if he wants to," she said. Then with a smile, "Have you forgotten California already?"

Marshall gave her a grin in return.

"Nope, an' I don't intend to, neither," he replied. "Reckon California'll just hafta wait a while longer f'r me, that's all. Now, if yuh think it's awright, I'll take a look aroun' outside an' kinda get th' feel o' things."

"Please do," Stella said brightly.

Marshall nodded, turned and strode out. The door closed quietly behind him. Stella smiled and strolled to the window. June dared not raise her eyes; she gave all her attention to the coffee.

"He's awfully good-looking," she heard Stella say, "isn't he?"

There was no comment from June.

"I wonder why some woman hasn't taken notice of it and done something about it," Stella went on.

She came away from the window. There was a curious, thoughtful smile on her face. June finally raised her eyes. Stella smoothed back her hair and ran her hands down along her skirt, smoothing that down, too. She turned slowly, still smiling, and went out.

It was late afternoon of the second day of Marshall's "hiring out" to the Circle D.

It was a bleak, chilly afternoon of a long, dismal day, one that had begun with an overcast sky and that had borne a day-long threat of rain. Actually, the threat had materialized; it had drizzled twice during the early afternoon. Fortunately neither sprinkling had lasted more than but a few minutes. But the threat still persisted. Now the sky was even darker, an ominous harbinger, and the prospect of real rain of longer duration was no longer a matter of conjecture. More and more black, low-hanging clouds appeared until the sky seemed to be filled to overflowing.

Marshall had ridden northward, a mile, perhaps two, beyond the grazing Davis herd. He checked the black, slowed him to a jog and finally halted. He relaxed wearily in the saddle, shifted himself a bit and winced when his cramped body protested. A sharp wind arose, and he whipped up the collar of his jacket and buttoned it securely around his neck. Dust swirled about in the wake of the wind, and he tugged at the brim of his hat and pulled it down over his eyes.

"H'm," he muttered. "Shore gonna be a mean night awright."

He wheeled the black and looked up when he felt a drop of rain.

"Uh-huh," he said aloud. "Here she comes."

"She" came shortly, a cold, chilling drizzle that obscured the range, the mountains and the river. Then the rain grew in intensity, and far away a mighty roar of thunder burst and echoed in a series of second-long, rolling explosions. He spurred the black and sent him bounding away southward. The big horse swept over the range at a swift pace, and soon Marshall heard the lowing of cattle; presently, ahead of him, he made out the herded forms of steers. In the swirling rain he spied three mounted men and rode toward them.

"That you, Marshall?" one of them called.

"Yep," he answered briefly, and pulled up.

The Circle D punchers clattered up and drew rein too.

"What about t'night?" a man asked. "Looks like it's gonna be meaner'n hell. Figurin' on keepin' all of us out here?"

"What for?" another man demanded. "Lookit that rain, willya? It's comin' down in buckets! Yuh don't s'ppose anyb'dy'd be loco enough t' pick a night like this un's gonna be t' run off some steers, do yuh? Hell, even a rustler knows enough t' stay in outa th' rain!"

"Uh-huh," the third man added. "Hank, I think yuh got somethin' there."

"Yuh do, eh?" Marshall snapped. "I c'n see you fellers don't know much about rustlers. Wa-al, I know plenty about 'em. I've tangled with 'em more'n once, an' I've learned things fr'm 'em. F'r one thing, this kind o' night is made t' order for 'em. They know that most folks are gonna hustle t' get under cover. But does that mean that they are too—th' rustlers, I mean? Hell, no. They'll be out t'night, yuh c'n d'pend on that—an' they'll find easier pickin's than ever."

"Yeah," the man named Hank admitted begrudgingly. "I s'ppose so."

"Awright then. So we're gonna ride herd t'night, an' what's more, we're gonna be on th' job every danged minute o' th' night. There's gonna be no soldierin'—savvy?"

There was no reply, no comment.

"Now then, couple o' yuh head f'r th' shack," he went on. "Get yore fill o' grub an' plenty o' hot coffee, then hustle back here. We'll eat in shifts so's none of us'll get th' worst or th' best of it. You, partner—what's th' rest o' yore name?"

"Who d'yuh mean—me?" Hank asked.

"Uh-huh."

"It's Hank—Hank Denning."

"An' yores, Mister?"

"I'm Steve Landon."

"Awright—you two fellers c'n go first. When yuh get back, we—oh, yeah, yore name's Lee, ain't it?"

The man who had hailed him grinned.

"Not unless it's been changed," he answered lightly. "It used t' be Dee—Dee Miles."

Marshall grinned back at him.

"If that's what it was b'fore, reckon it still is," he said. "Like I started t' say, when you fellers get back, Dee here an' me'll go get us some grub."

"Want us t' go now?" Denning asked.

"Might's well," Marshall said briefly.

"S'awright with me," Landon said, and looked at Denning.

"Let's go," the latter said.

He wheeled his horse. Landon followed. They spurred their mounts and dashed away toward the river. It was suddenly evening, and the enveloping darkness and the swirling rain swallowed them up. Marshall turned in his saddle and looked after them. Charley Davis, he had already learned, had erected a shack and a connecting lean-to close to the river bank. The shack had been intended to serve as a tool storehouse, but shortly after it was built Davis himself was forced to take refuge in it when he was caught in a sudden storm. The warmth and the safety that the shack afforded were all he could have desired; it was the lack of food that had finally forced him to abandon the shack and venture out and make the long, hazardous trek home.

From then on Davis had ordered that food be cached in the shack, and that the supply be watched faithfully and promptly replenished whenever it appeared to be dwindling. From then on, too, the men who rode herd over the Circle D steers had made the shack their headquarters.

Marshall settled himself in his saddle. He disregarded the rain that beat against his face and glanced at his waiting companion.

"Dee," he began.

Miles edged his mount closer.

"Yeah?"

"There ain't much chance o' anybody bustin' in on us fr'm any d'rection but fr'm th' north," Marshall went on. "I'm gonna ride up there. S'ppose you go join Denning an' Landon, an' when th' three o' yuh get back, I'll go eat."

"Whatever yuh say, Marshall," Dee answered, "on'y I don't like leavin' yuh out here by y'self."

"Heck, I'll be awright. It's too early f'r anythin' excitin' t' happen. But, if anythin' does pop—tell yuh what, Dee—if I see anythin' that don't look just right I'll fire a couple o' warnin' shots, pronto, too, an' you fellers c'n hotfoot it up here t' join me. That awright?"

"Wa-al, yeah, I s'ppose so. But yuh better watch y'self anyway, Marshall."

"Don't worry about that," Marshall said grimly.

"I'll kinda hustle th' boys along," Miles continued, "so's yuh won't be stuck out here by y'self any longer'n necessary."

"Swell."

Miles hesitated for a moment, then finally wheeled his horse.

"See yuh soon," he called over his shoulder.

"You bet."

Dee galloped off. After he had gone Marshall rode slowly northward. The lowing cattle were nervous and restless. The black broke into a canter and swung along the fringe of the herd. The steers shied away hastily, trampling one another in their alarm and fright. Quickly Marshall swerved the big horse, spurred him and sent him bounding away. They swept over the soggy turf at a swift pace; minutes later they had left the herd behind them. A quarter of a mile away Marshall checked the black, slowed him to a trot and finally pulled him to a halt.

Marshall looked about him. He could see nothing through the solid curtain of rain. He shook his head.

"Lookit it come down!" he said half aloud. "Bet it couldn't rain 'ny harder if it wanted to!"

He shifted himself in the saddle and winced as before. He kicked his feet free of the stirrups and allowed them to dangle. When he bent his head, a stream of water ran down the brim of his hat and splashed against his jacket front.

"Damn," he said thickly.

The black pawed the soggy ground impatiently. Marshall looked up.

"What's eatin' you?" he demanded gruffly. "You ain't th' on'y one gettin' soaked, y'know. Just b'cause I'm sittin' up here don't mean I'm keepin' dry."

The black snorted in reply.

"It shore beats all," Marshall muttered, "how I c'n get into things. Seems like folks just about save up their troubles till I come along; then they kinda dump 'em into my lap an' leave it t' me t' straighten things out f'r 'em. I'm gonna get t' hate folks, danged if I'm not. One o' these fine days I'm simply gonna head f'r th' mountains, find me a place that nob'dy c'n get to an' stay put there. Yep, that's just what I'm gonna do."

The black snorted again, a snort that sounded unusually like a cynical laugh. Marshall glared at him.

"Yeah? Wa-al, just wait. Reckon I'll show you a couple o' things, too."

He shook his head sadly, and settled himself deeper in the saddle. He wheeled the black and rode westward again. He stiffened in the saddle when he heard hoof beats, and jerked the big horse to an abrupt halt. The echo of hoof beats grew louder. He loosened the Colt in its holster on his right thigh, his hand ready for an instant draw.

"Marshall!" a voice cried.

He recognized the voice—it was Dee's. He spurred the black and rode forward again at a swift pace. Dee came cantering up through the chill rain.

"Hi, feller!" he yelled. "Yuh awright?"

" 'Course. Yuh done eatin'?"

"Yep. Hank an' Steve are finished too. Hank's ridin' south 'long th' river bank; then he's gonna swing aroun' th' herd. Steve's comin' this way. You'll prob'bly run into 'im," Dee answered.

"Swell. Dee, you an' Steve better stick t'gether. I'll hustle back soon's I c'n; then we'll all kinda spread out."

"Whatever yuh say, Marshall. Yuh're th' boss, y'know. On'y there ain't no reason f'r yuh t' hustle back. Yuh must be soaked as well as hungry, so take yore time. Reckon th' three of us oughta be able t' hold th' fort."

Marshall swung the black around.

"Watch out f'r y'self," he said.

The big horse dashed away. Marshall heard hoof beats again and saw a shadowy horseman coming toward him. Marshall swung in closer toward the approaching rider; when they came abreast of each other, both skidded to a halt.

"That you, Steve?" he called.

"Yep," came Landon's prompt reply. "Yuh see Dee?"

"Yeah, just left 'im. He's waitin' back there f'r yuh," Marshall said, turning and pointing. "See yuh later."

Steve galloped off. Marshall loped away toward the shack. He swung south when he reached the river bank. Minutes later he spied a shadowy structure looming up ahead of him. It was the shack. He swerved a bit and pulled up in front of it. A faint yellowish light broke through the rain-spattered window and cast an eerie ray over the wet turf beneath it. Marshall dismounted, led the black into the lean-to and halted when he stumbled over an opened bag of oats. Something glistened beside it—a pan of water.

"There y'are, boy," Marshall said. "Dig in."

The black needed no coaxing. He "dug" into the oats with

a vengeance. He paused but once, to raise his head and whinny his delight, then went on eating. Marshall watched him for a moment, turned finally and permitted his eyes to range over the lean-to. It was a spacious and sturdily built affair, well roofed and equally well walled, with sufficient room for half a dozen horses. There was a curious stirring and a strange movement from a dark far corner, and another horse suddenly plodded forward. Marshall looked sharply at the animal, then decided that it was probably a "spare" kept there in case of an emergency. The newcomer crowded against the black. The latter looked up and snorted angrily, and the second horse hastily retreated. Marshall grinned. There was a door close by; he opened it and found himself looking into the shack itself.

There was warmth in the shack and a pleasant fragrance of fresh coffee in the warm air.

"Uh-m-m," he muttered. "Shore smells good."

Marshall's eager eyes sought the coffee pot. He spied a heavy iron pail beneath a crude makeshift table, strode over and looked down. There were glowing embers in the bottom of the pail, and a somewhat battered and discolored coffee pot rested on an improvised grill that had been fashioned across the mouth of the pail. A tiny wisp of steam curled lazily upward from the pot.

He whipped off his hat and dropped it on one of the boxes, unbuttoned his jacket and took it off. There was a barrel in a far corner, and he strode over to it, intending to drape his jacket over it. Instead, he halted midway and stared hard. A slim figure that had been crouching beside the barrel came erect. It was Stella.

CHAPTER 13

JUNE TURNED down the light in the lamp that stood on the kitchen table. She went to the door and tried it. She unlocked it and snapped the bolt home, drew it back and snapped it shut a second time before she appeared satisfied that it would really hold. The upper panel of the door was a curtained pane of glass. She pushed the short curtain aside, shaded her eyes with her hands and peered out. Huge raindrops spattered against the pane and distorted her view. She drew the curtain back into place, turned away and trudged off, only to halt again when she came abreast of the room's only window. Here too she tried the lock—Davis had equipped the outer doors and the windows with sturdy slide bolt locks—made certain that it was secure and drew down the blind.

Then she made her way to her room, shut the door and snapped the lock with a single twist of her wrist. Curiously enough, hers was the only door aside from the outer doors that boasted of a lock. She had had occasion to go to her room earlier; she was glad now that she had forgotten to turn out the light, glad too that she had locked her window, even though she had done it mechanically then and without cause. It was a simple matter now to step to the window and pull down the blind and thus assure herself of complete privacy. She sank back against the door and breathed a deep sigh of relief.

After a few minutes she straightened up, strode to the bed and threw back the covers. She whisked her nightgown out of a bureau drawer and started to undress when she suddenly realized that the room was chilly and damp. She quickened her undressing and slipped into the gown and turned toward the bed again, only to halt with a pout. She hadn't lowered the lamp light. She retraced her steps, and snapped off the light completely before she could check herself. She was too cold to bother lighting it again, and a third time she turned toward the bed. She reached it stumblingly, climbed in and gasped aloud when her bare feet touched the sheets. They were icy. She slid down trembling, drew up her knees and burrowed deep into the bed, even pulled the covers over her head.

Presently she felt warmer, uncovered her head, settled herself a bit more comfortably and closed her eyes, hoping that sleep would come without delay. But sleep did not come, at least not as quickly as she had hoped. She turned on her side, then on her back, lying still when she heard the rain carom off the window and the side of the house, heard it patter with lightning steps over the roof. The window rattled beneath the sudden onslaught of a sharp gust of wind, and it frightened her.

When she heard something outside her window she became still more frightened, for it wasn't just the rain. This was something different—it was a strange sort of tapping on the window pane.

For a moment she lay rigidly still. Again she heard the tapping, perhaps a bit louder this time than before. She was tempted to scream; in fact she just about managed to stifle a scream which arose in her throat. She looked about her frantically, but she realized at once that there was no one there to help her. Suddenly her curiosity overcame her fear, and she slipped out of bed and tiptoed to the window. The tapping reached its highest pitch just as she reached the window. Cautiously she drew back the edge of the blind and peered out. There was a man out there, his face almost pressed against the pane, and he was staring up at her from beneath the brim of his rain-drenched hat!

June gasped. There was a sudden, frightening crash of thunder and an equally sudden and brief second-long flash of lightning, and she saw the man's face. It was the Sheriff, Sam Barnes! He seemed to have recognized her too, for he backed away from the window with all possible haste and stared up at her, wide-eyed. There was another crash of thunder, and he wheeled and fled while June dropped the blind with the haste of a man who has picked up a red hot coal and who decides in that same moment to get rid of it. Then she turned and dashed back to bed, jumped in and pulled the covers over her head.

"Hello," Stella said brightly. "Lovely evening, isn't it?"

"Howdy," Marshall replied. "What's so lovely about it? Where I was up to a couple o' minutes ago it was kinda wet an' cold an' not p'rticularly lovely—leastways not so's I could notice. Lose yore way?"

"No."

He laid his jacket on an upended box.

"This what yuh allus do—keep tabs on yore hired hands, day an' night?"

"No, not exactly."

"Then what are yuh doin' out here on a night like this?"

She smiled and dimpled.

"Maybe I came to see you."

He laughed easily.

"Yeah, mebbe."

"It happens that I did come to see you," she said quietly. "Aren't you glad?"

"Oh, I dunno. Think I oughta be?"

"I'll leave that to you to decide."

He turned away, found a cup in a small cupboard on the wall behind him, poured himself a cup of coffee and slowly drank it. She watched him quietly, patiently. He filled the cup a second time and drank its contents even more slowly than he had the first. Finally he put down the cup and picked up his jacket.

"You're going so soon?"

He slipped into the jacket and buttoned it up.

"Yep. Can't expect th' other men t' stay out there while I stay in here, y'know."

She moved along the edge of the table and halted within arm's reach of him.

"You don't like me, Marshall, do you?"

"Oh, I wouldn't say that."

"Then what would you say?"

He looked down at her for a moment, his hands jammed deep into the pockets of his jacket; he studied her carefully through steady, calmly appraising eyes. She was motionless before him.

"Well?"

"Dunno," he said, and added a boyish grin.

"Afraid to commit yourself?"

"No, not exactly."

"You're afraid of me, Marshall, aren't you?"

"Nope."

"I think you are. If you weren't, you wouldn't be in such a hurry to go."

He grinned again.

"Awright, just t' prove t' yuh that yuh're dead wrong—" he unbuttoned his jacket—"I'll stay a while longer."

She laughed softly.

"Thanks. I like a man who isn't afraid."

"That so? I like a woman who is afraid—that's th' way a woman's s'pposed t' be."

She laughed again and moved a bit closer to him.

"We could be very good friends, Marshall," she said quietly. "I'd soon make you forget you'd ever heard of California, or that you'd ever wanted to go there."

He grinned and shook his head.

"I don't think so."

She threw her arms around him suddenly. They tightened around his neck, and she kissed him full on the mouth.

"Well?" she demanded smilingly. "Do you still doubt it?"

"Wa-al what?" he echoed calmly, ruthlessly, with a trace of mockery in his voice. "I've been kissed b'fore, y'know."

She frowned and lowered her arms. She was completely taken back—his unresponsiveness gave her a severe jolt. She was suddenly aware that she had made a fool of herself and sensed that behind his calmness he was laughing at her. She had goaded him into staying; he had done exactly as she had wished, yet now she wished that he had gone, wished too that she had never come. She was furious with herself. Then something flamed within her, an idea born of anger and of woman's first emotion—jealousy. She knew in an instant why he hadn't succumbed—it was because of June.

There was but one thought in her mind, now that she had discovered the cause for her failure, and that one thought demanded immediate action. She bolted past Marshall, flung open the door and raced out. He turned, followed her to the door, halted in the open doorway and watched. The black looked up when he heard Stella's fleet step, whinnied and edged forward to meet her. She came abreast of him and struck at him. He snorted and quickly backed away. She reached her own horse, mounted, clattered out of the lean-to and disappeared into the rainy darkness.

For a brief moment her horse's hoof beats could be heard over the downpour; then they were gone, faded into the steady overwhelming downbeat of the rain. Marshall shook his head. Women were a curious lot. He made a wry face and wiped his mouth hard with the back of his hand.

"Danged fool," he muttered.

He buttoned up his jacket, looked back over his shoulder, spied his hat resting on the very edge of one of the boxes and went back for it, clapped it on his head and turned again toward the door only to halt and scowl at the lamp. He debated with himself whether to leave it as it was or to turn the light down. He decided finally to leave it untouched. Doubtless someone would want more coffee later on; then the men would be wandering back to the shack again. He trudged out, pulling the door shut behind him.

The black trotted forward again, halted in front of him and rubbed his nose against Marshall's shoulder. Marshall patted the horse's sleek neck affectionately.

"So she took her mad out on you too, eh?"

The black whinnied softly.

"Wa-al, she'll get over it. But if she don't, I reckon we'll still be able t' bear up under it, won't we, huh?"

The black whinnied in agreement.

Marshall gripped the reins and vaulted up into the saddle. Slowly they rode out of the lean-to and into the driving rain.

It was cold and dismal in the huge darkened barn, and the rain pounded against the gabled roof and caromed off the planked walls without a let-up. Pecos scowled, mumbled to himself and huddled deeper into the old blanket he had been provided with. He sank down and buried his face in the folds of the blanket, then jerked his head up again, for there was a foul smell about the blanket. Finally he cast it off completely.

"Hey!" he yelled.

From the shadowy darkness at the front of the barn came a prompt acknowledgment.

"Shut up, yuh polecat!"

Pecos strained at the ropes which bound his wrists behind him. If only he could free himself for just one minute— He struggled, but in vain, and finally subsided. He pushed back into the very corner of the stall, seeking the protection of the stall walls against the cold. He saw the shadowy figure of the puncher who had been detailed to guard him arise. Pecos scowled as he watched him spread his blankets on the hay-strewn floor. The man rolled himself up in his blankets and pushed himself forward until he came to rest directly against the door. No one—and Pecos acknowledged it freely—could open the door without arousing the guard.

Presently there was a stirring among the horses.

86

"Settle down there, will yuh?" the guard yelled.

The horses quickly subsided. Then a shadowy figure suddenly rose in front of Pecos, who gulped and swallowed hard.

"Sh," came the whispered warning.

Pecos tried to answer, but somehow nothing resulted from his efforts; then the newcomer was at his side.

"The girl—" a voice whispered into his ear—Pecos recognized the voice as that of a woman—"the girl's alone in the house. Keep quiet and do exactly as I say and I'll get you out of here."

Pecos grunted in reply.

"You'll have to crawl," the voice added. Pecos knew the voice now—it was Stella's.

"My hands are tied b'hind m' back," he whispered. "C'n yuh do somethin' 'bout 'em?"

"Yes—bend forward."

Pecos obeyed with alacrity. Stella inched past him. He felt the chilling steel of a knife, felt it cut into the rope; then his wrists were free.

"All right?" Stella asked. "Come on, now—follow me."

She crept out of the stall, lower now, on hands and knees, with Pecos at her very heels. They headed toward the rear of the barn, making their way through tall mounds of hay and countless stacked bags of feed. Pecos heard the faint creak of a door. A cold wind suddenly struck him, and he winced.

"Come on!" Stella whispered over her shoulder.

In another moment they were out of the barn and into the rainy night. Pecos scrambled to his feet. Stella darted off. Pecos bounded after her and caught up with her. When she motioned him away frantically, he twisted away and fell in behind her. They raced along the length of the towering barn, keeping well within the shadows it threw off. When Stella swerved away and headed toward a group of trees, Pecos swung away sharply too, followed her through the trees and panted up behind her to the kitchen door. Pecos noticed that there were faint lights in many of the windows of the ranchhouse.

"The door's open," Stella whispered. "Go through the kitchen, turn right through an open doorway, turn right again when you come to the hallway. Her room's at the very end of it."

"Awright," Pecos grunted. "What do I do then?"

"I've unlocked her door," Stella continued. "She's asleep. You'll have to get her out quickly and, above all, quietly."

"Go on."

"I've got a horse waiting for you. He's back there in the bushes. If you work fast, you'll get away safely—otherwise—"

"There ain't gonna be no otherwise," Pecos said sharply. "Tell me—what's th' big idea b'hind all this? How come yuh're doin' this?"

Stella bristled.

"I'm doing you a favor," she snapped. "Take advantage of it."

Pecos' white teeth gleamed in the darkness.

"I aim to," he said quickly. "An' thanks."

"See to it that you don't talk," Stella added curtly.

"I won't," Pecos answered. "Yuh c'n d'pend on that."

"All right then," Stella said finally. "Go ahead."

Pecos hitched up his pants, opened the door and stepped inside. He halted in the doorway and listened, then, apparently satisfied that it was safe to continue, plodded away. Stella quickly withdrew into the enveloping darkness. She reappeared presently, leading a saddled horse, halted him again just outside the door and promptly retreated. She crouched down behind a clump of brush and waited. The minutes dragged by, and with each minute's passing she grew more impatient and more nervous, fearful lest someone might appear.

Then Pecos finally emerged. Stella half arose and caught her breath and stared hard. There was a blanket-covered, struggling figure in his arms—a barelegged figure that fought frantically to free herself from the blanket that had been thrown over her head. Pecos shifted his burden to his left arm, gripped the bridle with his free hand and pulled himself up into the saddle. He settled his captive within his encircling left arm, wheeled the horse and loped off.

Stella, trembling with excitement, listened intently, but the retreating hoofbeats quickly faded out. She drew a deep breath, straightened up finally, turned and tramped farther back into the darkness. She led out another horse—her own—climbed up into the saddle, rode around the house and reined in at the front door. After a minute she spurred away and loped past the bunkhouse and the corral and pulled up in front of the barn. She dismounted and strode up to the door, but she made no attempt to open it—instead, she rapped on it loudly. There was no response. She knocked a second time. After a few minutes the door was opened, and a man poked his head out.

"Wa-al?" he demanded irritably. "What in blazes d'yuh want, dang yuh?"

"Why, Johnny—"

The man blinked and stared up at her. He rubbed his heavy eyes and looked hard at her a second time.

"Oh, h'llo, Stella," he said sheepishly, and managed a feeble laugh. "Thought you were one o' th' boys, an' I was all set t' jump down yore throat. They're th' doggonedest bunch o' galoots I ever knowed—they're allus up t' somethin'."

Stella laughed lightly.

"I see. I'm sorry I had to wake you."

Johnny dismissed her apology with a wave of his hand.

"Shucks, Stella, f'rget it," he said quickly. "Some night, huh?"

"Awful, Johnny, awful."

"Yep, an' am I glad I didn't hafta ride herd t'night!"

"Johnny, will you put my horse away, please?"

"'Course."

He swung the door wide and stepped outside, caught the bridle of Stella's horse and led him into the barn.

"Thanks, Johnny," Stella said. "Good night."

"G'night, Stella," he called over his shoulder.

Stella turned and plodded off toward the house. Midway she heard the barn door close. She reached her own front door presently, produced a key and, after a minute's fumbling with it at the lock, opened the door and stepped inside.

CHAPTER 14

STELLA'S SCREAMS brought the Circle D punchers pouring out of their bunkhouse on the double. A few of them were fully clad—others struggled to shove their flying shirt tails into the waistband of their pants as they ran along. They came thundering up to the ranchhouse just as Stella, a heavy coat thrown over her nightdress, ran out. They gathered around her quickly.

"June!" she gasped. "She's gone!"

"Huh? What d'yuh mean 'gone'?" a man asked. "Yuh shore she ain't in 'er bed?"

"She's gone, I tell you!" Stella almost screamed. "I looked in her room just a minute ago and she wasn't there!"

"Wa'al, what d'yuh know!"

"And the kitchen door," Stella continued breathlessly. "It was wide open!"

The men looked at each other questioningly.

"What d'yuh s'ppose we oughta do?"

"One of you," Stella said quickly, "go get Marshall!"

"Yeah, that's 'n idea."

One of the men turned without another word and raced away toward the barn. He hammered on the door, which was presently flung open. He disappeared inside, reappeared a minute or two later astride a saddled horse and came galloping up to the group in front of the house.

"Jake," a puncher called.

The mounted man twisted around in his saddle.

"Yeah?"

"If yuh don't find Marshall right off, don't waste no time ridin' aroun' lookin' f'r 'im. Head straight f'r th' shack. Like's not that's where he an' th' other boys'll be anyway."

Jake clattered away.

"What d'yuh say we get in somewheres outta this danged rain?" someone asked.

"Yeah, let's," another man added. "This rain's wet."

Stella turned and led the way into the house.

Marshall came slowly out of the house. The waiting black looked up expectantly, and when Marshall sauntered past him without so much as a glance in his direction, the big horse whinnied. Marshall halted and looked over at him, then trudged on again. Midway between the house and the corral he halted a second time, turned and retraced his steps and started around the house toward the rear.

He came to an abrupt stop when he spied something lying in the grass some eight or ten feet ahead of him. It gleamed

90

with a metallic brightness. He stared at it, then looked up, his eyes ranging along the windows on the side of the house. He was trying to locate June's window. Yes, there it was; that was her room. He looked down again quickly. The thing lay directly in front of her window. He strode forward, bent down, picked it up and turned it over in his hand. It was a silver star —a lawman's badge—and it bore a single word: "Sheriff." On the back of the star, just below the sturdy clasp, were two faint, pin-scratched initials. He held it up so that the night light, or what little there was of it, might shine on it.

"H'm—S. B.," he muttered after a minute's careful study "Reckon they're s'pposed t' stand f'r Sam Barnes. If this thing's really his, then it's th' first time I ever noticed that a feller's initials could give such a perfect d'scription of 'im."

He turned slowly, the star tightly gripped in his big hand.

"Sam Barnes," he mumbled. "Now what d'yuh s'ppose that polecat was doin' out here? An' while I'm still wonderin' out loud, what d'yuh s'ppose he had t' do with June an' her disappearance?"

He plodded out to the front of the house and halted again. He opened his fist and stared down at the star. He toyed with it for a moment, then suddenly shoved it into his pocket. He strode briskly over the soggy ground to the idling black and vaulted into the saddle.

"Let's go," he snapped. He settled himself and wheeled the big horse. "We gotta go see a man about a girl, so th' sooner we see th' polecat, th' sooner we're gonna know where she's at. Go 'head, boy!"

The black thundered away.

Sam Barnes yawned and stretched and shifted himself in his chair. He swung his legs up and propped them on the edge of the desk. He looked ceilingward and frowned—the dim light in the office was annoying. He eyed the lamp that hung from the ceiling and cursed it under his breath. It gave a poor light, and the barest bit of vibration usually caused it to sway so that Sam fully expected it to tear itself loose from the bolts that held it in place and come crashing down. It hadn't been right since the night that fool in the black garb had shot up the place, when the lamp had been gun-blasted to the floor. Sam had tried to fix it up, but he wasn't much of a hand at such things. He gave a fleeting thought to Marshall—wondered what had become of him—and just as promptly forgot about him.

For a moment Sam debated with himself whether to go across to the Cafe for a drink, and the longer he pondered the matter the more appealing the thought of a drink became. He made up his mind finally, turned on his heel, strode to the rear of the office and into the tiny room behind it, donned his hat and coat and came striding out again. He opened the street door—the rain was coming down heavily. He stepped out and pulled the door shut behind him—he had already decided it was unnecessary to lock it since he wouldn't be gone more than a few minutes. He lowered his head and darted across the street.

It was about five minutes later when Sam returned to the office. He locked the door behind him, whipped off his coat and hat and carried them to the rear. Then he jerked to an abrupt, awkward halt when a tall figure, gun in hand, suddenly stepped out in front of him. Sam gulped and blinked. The muzzle of Marshall's big Colt gaped hungrily at Sam's ample stomach.

"Awright, Barnes—drop them things an' sit down," Marshall ordered.

He backed a bit to allow the Sheriff to pass.

"C'mon," he snapped impatiently when Sam hesitated. He waved him on with his gun, and Sam finally edged past him, nervously and falteringly, and dropped his coat and hat on a nearby chair. "Sit down there."

Sam seated himself gingerly, almost on the very edge of the chair.

"Now, Mister, talk."

"What—what about?"

Marshall's eyes glinted.

"Th' weather, if yuh like," he said grimly, "on'y if I was you I'd get right down t' cases an' b'gin with somethin' about th' Circle D. An' don't take too long. I'm 'n impatient gent, an' m' trigger-finger gets itchy an' nervous when it has t' wait."

Sam swallowed hard. The muzzle of the Colt seemed to widen the longer he stared at it—now it seemed to have swelled to the bursting point.

"Oh, yeah," Marshall said suddenly. He dug into his jacket

92

pocket, pulled out the silver star and tossed it into Sam's hands. "Ever see that b'fore?"

Sam stared hard at it, and suddenly clutched at his shirt front. When he drew his hand away and found it empty, he seemed dazed. He raised his head. There was a strange expression on his blood-drained face—incredulity—He seemed unable to understand how he had lost it and even more stunned at his own failure to notice its loss before this. Now his face was a pasty, greenish white.

"Where—where'd yuh find this?" he managed to ask in a voice that seemed strange, even to Marshall.

"Where yuh lost it," the latter said gruffly. "You oughta know where that was."

"Musta been at th' Circle D," Sam mumbled.

"'Course. What'd yuh do with June Halliday?"

Sam's eyes bulged.

"Who—me? I saw 'er," he sputtered protestingly, "but that's all."

"Where'd yuh see 'er?"

"She was standin' at a window, lookin' out."

"What'd yuh go t' th' Circle D for?"

Sam flushed uneasily.

"Now that's pers'nal," he protested again, lamely. "It didn't have nuthin' t' do with June—honest it didn't."

Marshall's long left arm shot out. He grabbed Sam by the shirt front and dragged him to his feet.

"Listen t' me, yuh polecat!" he gritted through clenched teeth. "When I ask yuh a question, answer it—understand? If yuh don't, I'll blast it outta yuh! Now start talkin', an' b'gin at th' b'ginnin', too, an' make damn sure yuh don't leave anythin' out either, even what yuh think is personal!"

He shoved Sam away roughly. Sam fell back into his chair so violently that it nearly tipped over. He looked up again presently, panting a bit, his face deathly white.

"Wa-al?"

Sam drew a deep breath.

"I—I went t' th' Circle D t' see Stella," he began nervously. Marshall eyed him sharply, almost unbelievingly.

"Stella?" he echoed. "Are you tryin' t' tell me that you an' Stella've been—"

Sam flushed and nodded slowly and averted his eyes.

"I'll be damned!" Marshall said softly. "She don't seem t' care a hoot who she gets tangled up with, does she, long's it's a man, eh? How long's this bus'ness been goin' on b'tween you an' Stella?"

"Oh, 'bout a month."

"An' how often yuh been seein' each other?"

"Couple o' times a week."

"Where?"

"Aroun' th' ranch, mostly."

"When?" Marshall demanded. "At night, I s'ppose, eh?"

The Sheriff nodded.

"Yeah," he said dully. "She'd slip outta th' house 'long about nine o'clock. I'd be waitin' f'r 'er, back a ways fr'm th' house, where all that brush is."

Marshall nodded as he listened. At the same time his thoughts were doubling back to the night of Charley Davis' killing. Everything came back to him, the events which had led up to it and those which had followed, clearly, concisely, orderly, as vividly as though they had just been reenacted.

He saw himself bending over the crumpled body of young Tom Haley; he recalled how he had looked up when the shot rang out and how he had instantly placed it as having been fired from the rear of the house; he saw himself sprinting forward toward the rear, remembered how he had skidded to a halt when he'd come upon Stella. He had a clear picture of her, kneeling beside the outstretched body of a man—Charley Davis—and screaming and sobbing. He recalled how he'd slipped past her, undetected—how he'd taken refuge behind a nearby clump of brush. Now he realized that it must have been the very same spot that Sam had been talking about!

Now, in his mind's eye, he saw Sam crouching behind the brush, a pudgy, wide-eyed man, panicky, perhaps terror-stricken, aware that Davis had discovered his presence. He could even picture the irate rancher striding toward the brush with Sam trying to back away, turning frantically this way and that, looking for a means of escape. But there was none—Davis was hurling himself at Sam. The Sheriff's gun jerked upward out of his holster—there was a single shot. There was no missing that lunging target, for Davis now was only inches away. There was a blinding flash and a loud roar. Davis' hands fell short. Mortally wounded, he halted, staggered back, spun on crumpling, buckling legs, and finally crashed over, dead before he struck the ground.

It was small wonder then that Haley's gun hadn't smelled of burnt gunpowder, but there was still a puzzling question in Marshall's mind: Why had Stella snatched up the youth's gun? If it had been her purpose to use it on her husband, or if she had intended only to bluff him with it—he, Marshall, would never know. Now the scene became a bit dimmed; the play was over and the last curtain was being lowered. He was back in the Sheriff's office and the Sheriff was staring at him, wondering at his silence.

"Barnes," Marshall began, "what d'yuh s'ppose is gonna happen when folks find out that it was you, th' Sheriff, who was monkeyin' aroun' with another man's wife, and that it was you who killed that man—huh? Hell—they'll prob'bly hang yuh higher'n a kite!"

Sam recoiled.

"Yuh mustn't tell 'em!" he gasped. "Yuh mustn't—yuh hear! I didn't mean t' kill Charley—honest I didn't! I didn't know what I was doin'. It was 'n accident—that's what it was, 'n accident!"

He bounded out of his chair, plunged forward to his knees and threw his arms around Marshall's legs and clung to them.

"Yuh gotta b'lieve me," Sam sobbed. "I'll do anythin' yuh say t' square it, on'y promise me that yuh won't tell 'nybody!"

Marshall broke Sam's hold on him and pushed him away roughly. He looked down at the sobbing man and shook his head.

"I'm sorry f'r yuh, Barnes," he said.

He holstered his gun, turned and strode swiftly to the street door and flung it open. Rain blew into the office. Marshall turned up the collar of his jacket.

"Wait!" he heard Sam cry.

He looked back over his shoulder. Sam Barnes, crouching a bit, a rifle gripped tightly in his hands, was framed in the doorway of the back room.

"Yuh gotta swear," Sam said thickly, "that yuh'll never tell 'nybody. If yuh don't—s' help me—I'll kill yuh!"

Marshall made no reply. He pulled down the brim of his hat and stepped out, halted and turned and reached for the door knob, intending to pull the door shut. Out of the corner of his eye he saw the rifle leap upward. His right hand streaked toward his holster.

There were two deafening claps of thunder, both almost blended into one, for there was practically no lapse of time between them—the heavy, authoritative voice of the Colt and the sharper, decisive crack of the rifle. Smoke filled the office. For a moment—it seemed an eternity—there was a breathtaking silence. A man's wearied sigh finally broke the stillness, a gun clattered harmlessly to the floor, then a body crashed heavily. The smoke lifted gently ceilingward, as though an unseen hand had wafted the obscuring veil away.

Face downward, or nearly so, on the floor, lay Sam Barnes, his right arm outflung, his left arm beneath him. His rifle lay inches beyond his right hand. Marshall glanced at him fleetingly, shook his head and holstered his gun. He took off his hat. There was a bullet hole in it, half-way up the crown. An inch lower and—Marshall disliked conjectures, and he quickly clapped the hat on his head, turned and trudged out. The door swung slowly, of its own accord, and closed behind him.

He was a hundred feet away when a couple of men came out of the Angels' Cafe, looked over at the Sheriff's office and started across the street. One of the men spied him and yelled to him, but Marshall paid no attention to him. He trudged on. He had already mounted and was headed out of town when he heard a yell behind him. He twisted around in the saddle and looked back. Two men were running up the street, calling to him. He spoke to the black. The big horse quickened his pace and broke into a swift gallop. Soon they had left Paradise behind them. In another moment the darkness blotted it out from sight.

CHAPTER 15

THE BLANKETED FIGURE on the bed stirred slightly, sighed and presently opened her eyes. On the bureau opposite the bed was a brightly lighted lamp, and the glare was blinding.

June hastily turned her head away, even threw up one bared arm to shield her eyes from the dazzling light. For a moment she was puzzled. She remembered quite distinctly that she had turned out the light before she'd climbed into bed. Then, startled into sudden and complete wakefulness by the terrifying thought that someone else had turned up the light and might be watching her, waiting for her to awake.

She turned her head a bit for a quick glance about her. She was alone. Her eyes widened and her heart leaped, for she was home again; she was in her own room at the Bar JH!

She sat up quickly, looked down and seemed surprised to find that her ankles were bare—now she remembered that she'd had no opportunity to dress herself. There was a crimson welt around her ankles. She remembered that they'd been bound, and she realized that the welt was proof of how tightly the rope had been knotted. For the first time she noticed the blanket that covered her. She recognized it at once—it was the one she'd become accustomed to seeing spread over her bed at the Circle D. She cast off the blanket, swung her legs over the side of the bed and tiptoed to the door. She tried the knob. It turned easily, even noiselessly; however, the door did not open. It was locked from the outside.

She wheeled and raced to her closet, just beyond the bed itself. Quickly she threw open the door, jerked a dress off a hook and threw it on the bed. She bent down, caught up a pair of sturdy shoes and put them down near the bed. She turned to the bureau, halted first to lower the lamp light, then pulled open a long drawer, snatched up some other bits of wearing apparel, wheeled and ran back to the clothes closet. She stepped behind the closet door, stepped out of her nightgown and into her clothes, completing the transformation in less time than she'd ever taken before. As a final touch, she kicked the nightgown into the closet and closed the door.

She went to the window, raised a corner of the fully drawn blind and peered out. The pane was rain-spattered, and her vision was hampered and limited. She could see that it was still raining, but that was all. She tried the window; it was unlocked, but she could not budge it. It was maddening—but now she remembered that it always "stuck" in damp weather. She turned away slowly, heavy-hearted, but in that same moment she spied something under her bed and raced across

97

the room, slid down to her knees and dug under the bed. She backed out and straightened up again, a makeshift riding crop in her hand. She remembered that one of the Bar JH punchers had whittled it for her. She climbed quickly to her feet and went back to the window. She pushed aside the blind again and, using the crop as a lever, finally managed to raise the window. It left her breathless for a moment; however, the window was open. She took a deep breath, bent down and put her shoulder to the sash. It squeaked a bit, protestingly, but the window went up higher beneath her straining shoulder.

She whirled and went back to the closet, dug deep into its depths, reappeared with a heavy coat in her hands and quickly slipped into it, then raced forward again to the window. She poked her head out. It was raining hard, but there was no one in sight. She slid one leg over the window sill; it finally found the ledge beneath the window. She twisted around, pulled herself over the sill, and steadied herself on the narrow footing outside. There was another window probably six or eight feet away, but she caught a glimpse of a light from within and drew back. She looked up, and a better idea quickly formed in her mind. Her room was the last one on the floor. Just beyond it, to the right, was a rain gutter that began at the roof and ended on the ground below. She inched along the ledge slowly, found the gutter with frantic fingers, got a good grip and clung to it desperately. She was motionless for another moment, gathering her strength together, for she knew that what lay ahead of her would demand the utmost of her.

She drew a deep breath and started to climb. It had looked far easier, she admitted after the very first moment, than it actually was. Slowly, hand over hand and inch by inch, she went upward, gripping the gutter with fingers that threatened constantly to lose their hold, for the rain had made the pipe slippery and far more difficult to negotiate than ordinarily. She hugged it with her knees, pressing them together until they ached, found the barest bit of support for her toes among the broken bits of wet shingles, dug in, reached up along the gutter for another and higher hold, tightened her grip and pulled herself up.

It was slow and painful progress, but progress it was, and in her frenzied bid for freedom, no price was exorbitant.

Once or twice her toes slipped and she slid downward help-lessly, but each time something happened and she barely man-aged to save herself. Once it was her skirt that provided the safety check that saved her from a disastrous fall. It caught on the rough, outer edge of the gutter, and she hung there, sus-pended in midair, breathless, frightened beyond words. Fran-tically she clutched at the gutter, inched her way upward again and freed her skirt and went on. Another time a broken sec-tion of the gutter broke her fall—it had torn away from the wall, and jutted out like a platform. She stood up on it, hanging on to the rest of the piping with one hand, resting the other, then alternating; after a minute she went on again, disregard-ing her cut and bruised hands and almost benumbed fingers, and her protesting and aching arms and legs. As for the rain, she ignored it completely.

Her heart leaped a bit when she turned her head and noted that she had managed to reach a point some three feet above the top of her window. Another three feet would do it—the roof couldn't be more than that distance away. Grimly she dug in, and held tightly to the gutter with her left hand while her right hand slid upward. On and on she went, doggedly, deter-minedly; then suddenly her probing right hand, which she was using as a "trail breaker," found itself gripping the very edge of the roof. She clung to it happily, panting for breath, marshaling her last bit of strength for the final upward surge.

If only she hadn't worn that heavy coat! It held her back, weighted her down and made climbing doubly difficult; how-ever, there was no shedding it now. She tightened her grip on the edge of the roof, slid her left hand upward to join its mate, then, exerting herself to the very utmost, pulled herself up and over the edge and collapsed in a heap.

As she lay there fighting for breath, she wondered if she hadn't chosen the wrong avenue of escape as well as the most difficult; she wondered too if she wouldn't have fared better if she had slid to the ground instead and chanced detection there. The roof, she now realized, offered but limited escape; the ground offered unlimited opportunities. However, there would be men coming and going, and in order to avoid detec-tion on the ground she would have had to scurry about con-tinually, dodging this way, then that way, leaping frantically from cover to cover, never knowing which way to turn, never daring to relax. Then, too, when daylight came and her captor —she had already decided that it must be Pecos—discovered that she had escaped, the ranch would be searched, inch by inch, with nothing under which she might take refuge left untouched. Recapture would then be but a matter of time. Perhaps she had chosen wisely at that; perhaps the roof was the safest place after all.

But final escape, she realized and admitted, would not come as a result of her own doing. After all, there were limits to her enterprise and capabilities. She would have to have help.

If only Marshall knew where she was! If only there were some way of letting him know!

She climbed stiffly to her feet. There was a chimney on the other side of the roof, and she trudged over to it and squatted down beside it, twisted around and planted her back against it. She whipped up her coat collar and buried her chin in its comforting depths, drew up her knees and huddled closer against the chimney. The rain, wind-lashed again, broke on the chimney and swirled around her, leaving her untouched. Her eyes were heavy. They closed gently. She nodded once or twice, shifted herself a bit, folded her arms on her knees and pillowed her head in them. Presently she was asleep.

The keen-eared black whinnied a warning, and Marshall, looking up quickly, slowed him down a bit. Now he could hear the faint rhythm of approaching hoof beats. They grew louder presently. He listened to them for a moment, trying to locate them, then decided that they were coming from the south, from the direction of the Circle D. He halted the black finally and waited, his hand on his gun butt. Then, from out of the darkness and the rain, which had now begun to abate, came a galloping horseman. The oncoming horseman appeared to be heading townward. The black whinnied. Marshall jerked the reins viciously, rebukingly, but it was too late. The newcomer pulled his mount to a skidding halt, twisted around in his saddle and looked about him quickly, seeking to locate the source of the whinny. Despite the dimming night light and the filmy curtain of rain that tended to veil most things, or at least make them unrecognizable from a short distance, he finally spotted the waiting black and his rider, spurred his horse and came cantering up.

"That you there, Marshall?" he called.

Marshall's anger cooled. He recognized the voice—it was Dee Miles'.

"Yep," he replied. "Where d'yuh s'ppose yuh're goin'?"

Dee edged his mount closer.

"T' find you, doggone it," he said lightly.

"Yuh don't say," Marshall countered. "Thought I left you an' them other two fellers ridin' herd? How come yuh laid off?"

"Couple o' th' boys come down t' r'lieve us," Miles explained. "One o' them said he'd seen you ridin' away fr'm th' house, an' another made some r'mark about them just findin' out that that ornery Pecos galoot had busted outta th' barn an' got plumb away."

"Oh, yeah?"

"Uh-huh. Anyway, right off I kinda put two an' two t'gether an'—"

"An' d'cided that it musta been Pecos who kidnapped June —right?"

"Right. 'Course I knew you didn't know anythin' about it an'—"

"An' yuh d'cided that I oughta. Yuh were dead right about that, Dee, an' I'm obliged t' yuh f'r botherin' t' get word of it t' me. Pecos' gettin' away puts a diff'rent light on things, y'know."

"Yuh mean that it points t' on'y one place t' look f'r th' Halliday kid, don'tcha?"

"Uh-huh, an' that's where I'm goin', an' pronto."

"An' I'm goin' with yuh."

"Hol' on there a minute, Miles. This ain't got anythin' t' do with you. Like I said b'fore, I'm obliged t' yuh f'r doin' what yuh did, so s'ppose yuh leave things there, turn around an' head back f'r th' ranch an' climb outta them wet clothes. A night's sleep'll do yuh a heap o' good."

"There'll be other nights when I c'n sleep," the puncher retorted. "T'night I got things t' do, an' I aim t' do 'em—see?"

Marshall laughed.

"Shore—but how come all this sudden int'rest in June Halliday, Dee? You ain't been hidin' somethin' fr'm me, have yuh?"

"Wish I was, Marshall. She's a nice kid. B'sides, she ain't

101

got 'ny folks t' take 'er part now—men folks, I mean—so some-b'dy's gotta look out f'r 'er. You ain't anythin' to 'er, leastways no more'n I am, an' if yuh're willin' t' buck Jess Barnes an' them hellions o' his t' save 'er—reckon I'm willin' t', too."

Marshall was silent for a moment.

"Y'know, Dee," he began again shortly, "there's bound t' be gun play when we tangle with 'em, an' that kind o' shootin' is th' real thing—shootin' f'r keeps. Anyone who takes a hand in a thing like that has t' be pr'pared t' kill—or he gets killed —savvy?"

"Tryin' t' scare me outta goin' along with yuh?"

"Mebbe."

"I don't scare that easy."

Marshall shrugged his shoulder.

"Whatever yuh say, Dee. Reckon yuh're old enough t' know what yuh're doin'," he said with finality.

" 'Course. Don'tcha think we oughta get goin' now?"

Marshall wheeled the black. Dee ranged his mount along-side. Together they spurred away.

CHAPTER 16

THE HORSES were tethered together within the protective screen of a thick clump of brush; then the two men sprinted away. There was no fear of detection—the ground was soggy, soft and muddy as a result of the heavy rain; their thumping boot treads were completely cushioned and absorbed. They slackened their pace when they came within sight of the con-necting bridge, and slowed down to a trot. They could see the water in the moat, gleaming with a curious brightness in the night light. The wind suddenly arose, droning inland from the river, lashed and churned the water about; the water in turn swirled madly against the banks of the moat.

Dee Miles glanced at Marshall. He noticed for the first time that Marshall had slung two coils of rope over his shoulder.

"Whatcha lug them along f'r?" he asked, nodding toward the lariats.

"Huh? Oh, yuh mean these?"

"Uh-huh."

"I allus make it a point t' tote along a rope," the black-clad man replied. "Seems like I c'n allus find use f'r it somehow, specially when I'm goin' callin' on a feller that ain't hankerin' f'r comp'ny."

Dee laughed lightly.

"Y'mean like Jess Barnes?"

"Yeah—mebbe."

They halted now and looked sharply across the intervening span of water.

"See 'nything?"

"Nope," Dee replied. "Looks like ev'ryb'dy musta called it a day an' turned in."

"Hope so," Marshall said briefly.

They trudged on again, finally came to a point within a dozen feet of the bridge and halted for a second time.

"We'd better take it easy-like goin' over," Dee said, "so's we don't wake 'nybody."

"Don't worry 'bout that," Marshall answered. "Nob'dy's gonna hear us. We ain't goin' over th' bridge—we're goin' under it, just in case they've got someb'dy planted in among them big trees near th' entrance. If we were t' take our chances on th' bridge, shucks—one o' th' planks might be loose, an' it'd squeak under us an' give us away."

"Yeah, yuh might have somethin' there," Dee admitted. "Awright, Marshall—you lead th' way an' I'll tag along b'hind yuh."

"Shore—on'y watch yore step. It'll be dark down there an', like's not, slippery's hell. B'sides, somethin' tells me that water's cold."

Dee's reply took the form of a grunt. With Marshall in the lead, they started down the embankment. The swirling water lapped loudly and roughly against the moat's banks, straining to attain height, seemingly striving to reach something alive that it could engulf and swallow up. It was treacherous underfoot, for the grass was wet and slippery. Dee's feet suddenly shot out from under him, and down he went. Marshall, a bare step or two ahead of him, whirled and dug in, managing to brace himself just as the plunging, water-bound puncher came crashing into him. For a moment it appeared that both of them would go toppling into the water, for Miles' frantically threshing feet nearly uprooted Marshall's. But the latter stepped aside quickly, caught Dee by the collar and held him fast.

"Awright?" Marshall asked in a low voice.

"Doggone it," Dee began, sputtering, his voice rising.

"Sh-h-h!"

Dee grunted and climbed halfway to his feet. Marshall turned away, whirled again suddenly, grabbed Dee by the arm and fairly dragged him under the bridge.

"What in blazes—" Dee began.

"Listen!"

They crouched together beneath the stout planking, listening intently, hardly daring to breathe. They heard a step, the rasping sound of a heavy boot on gravel, the step of a sauntering man.

"He's comin' closer," Dee whispered.

In the darkness his right hand sought his gun butt, but Marshall's hand caught and gripped Dee's and jerked it away from his gun.

"Don't be a damned fool!" he gritted in Dee's ear. "That feller's on'y a guard, an' he's comin' out f'r a look aroun' like he's s'pposed to. When he's had it, he'll go back inside."

"I hope so," Miles muttered.

"Wa-al, just keep yore shirt on an' see if I ain't right," Marshall continued.

The sound of footsteps ceased.

"Y'see?" Marshall whispered. "He's stopped, ain't he? Awright then—in a minute he'll be turnin' aroun' an' goin' back."

There was no comment from Dee. It was less than a minute later when they heard the man's step again; but as Marshall had predicted, each footfall carried the man farther away from them until finally his retreating steps faded out altogether.

"There y'are," Marshall said. "He's gone."

Dee grunted and sank down on the ground.

"Wa-al," he began with a deep sigh of relief, "all I gotta say is that it's a damn good thing you heard 'im comin'. If yuh hadn't, reckon we'da been done f'r. What d'we do now, Marshall?"

"First thing you c'n do," Marshall answered, "is stand up, on'y watch yore head. Them logs an' planks are hard."

Dee climbed slowly to his feet, straightened up even more slowly.

"Awright, I'm up," he announced presently. "What now?"

"Put yore hand up over yore head. Easy, now! Feel that log—th' outside one?"

"Yep—it's thicker'n a man's head."

"Wa-al, d'yuh think if yuh got both o' yore hands around it, yuh could swing y'self clear across th' water to th' other side?" Marshall asked.

"Shore," came Dee's quick response. "That's easy."

"Yuh'll find it's a heap harder'n it looks. S'ppose yuh lemme go first, Dee? When I get across I'll sling yuh a rope. Yuh c'n tie it around yore middle. That's just in case somethin' happens. I'll be hangin' on t' th' other end o' th' rope an' I'll be able t' fish yuh out. Awright?"

"Yeah, shore—but s'ppose somethin' happens t' you, b'fore yuh reach th' other side?" Miles asked.

"Reckon I'll get wet."

Dee stepped aside. Marshall hitched up his pants, shifted his holsters a bit and reached up with both hands. His body swung off the ground, in another minute he was inching along the log, then he was over water. Dee, crouching on the bank, followed him with anxious eyes. Finally a grin appeared on his face. He shook his head.

"That feller's awright," he muttered. "He makes everything look easy."

He stared hard across the span of water and pulled away hastily when a lariat swished past his head. He lunged for it, caught it and snapped it up and tied it around his waist. He hitched up his pants as he had seen Marshall do, spat on his hands and reached overhead. His hands tightened instantly around the log. He jerked himself upward, off the ground.

"There," he said half aloud. "That'll show 'im."

Hand over hand he started swinging himself along the log. It wasn't particularly difficult at first—he was surprised, a bit pleased, too, at the ease with which he managed to move himself. Then suddenly he stopped. A strange feeling came over him. His body was suddenly dead weight, while his dangling legs—he couldn't even draw them up! They were leaden weights, lifeless and heavy. He was puzzled. Just a minute before he'd been all right—now, suddenly, he was exhausted. He scowled darkly, tightened his grip and managed with a desperate surge and a superhuman heave of his body to move a little. He was panting for breath now. He hung there for a minute, motionlessly, fighting for breath. He gritted his teeth, baring them wolfishly, breathing heavily through his nose and teeth with a curious hissing sound. He had lost all sense of feeling in his body and legs—everywhere save in his arms, and they had a strange tired numbness about them.

He twisted around a bit so that he could look down, bumped his head painfully against the unyielding log and cursed loudly. He was angry now, and he tried to swing himself along at a faster pace than before. He was over water, but how far out he could not tell. The rope round his waist jerked sharply.

"Doggone it!" he panted angrily. "What'n hell's—"

He tried to shift his hands, they slipped, he lunged frantically for the log again—and went plunging downward.

Marshall had jerked the line, not because he was getting impatient but as a warning to Dee. He had heard a step somewhere along the gravel path that wound upward and away from the bridge. It was probably the sauntering step of the guard; the man was evidently coming out for another "look around." Since the rope constituted his only means of communicating with Dee, Marshall had jerked it, only once and then sharply, hoping that the puncher would understand from the single pull on the line that someone was coming, and that it was warning to him to beware.

Marshall whirled as Dee struck the water. He whipped his end of the rope around one of the stubby uprights that helped support the bridge and jerked the line taut. Dee would be safe out there for a while anyway—at least until Marshall took care of the guard, whose appearances were becoming annoying. Marshall knotted the rope, stepped over the taut line and peered out cautiously. He heard the thump of running, booted feet and pulled back hastily. The shadowy figure of a man, rifle in hand, dashed past him to the water's edge. The man crouched there for a moment, rifle raised, staring at the struggling Dee in the swirling water of the moat.

Marshall came up silently behind the guard. He whipped out a big Colt and shifted it in his hand. It flashed upward;

then he brought it down hard, butt first, on the man's head. The rifle slid harmlessly to the ground. The man toppled and crashed over sideways. Marshall holstered his gun, bent over him, got a firm grip on his jacket collar and dragged him away.

He turned again toward the moat. The current had carried Dee past midstream, and he was threshing about furiously, struggling for all he was worth, for there was evidently a powerful undertow in the moat. Marshall quickly caught up the line and pulled hard.

Dee Miles came ashore presently, riding up the embankment on his stomach, panting and blowing like a whale. Marshall bent over him, untied the rope which Dee had looped around his waist, tossed it aside and dragged him away. There was no telling when other members of the gang might appear—no knowing when a relief guard might trudge out in search of the man whose post he would take over. When they were safely under the bridge again, Marshall knelt down beside the panting, waterlogged puncher.

"Dee, yuh awright?"

The puncher's chest stopped heaving. He took advantage of the opportunity to raise himself on his elbows, turned his dripping head and spat out a mouthful of water.

" 'Course I'm awright," he gasped. He grimaced and spat out some more water. "Just b'cause I swallered th' hull danged river an' mebbe a couple o' dozen fish don't mean 'nything. What of it if I on'y use water f'r washin' an' never f'r drinkin' an' if I don't like fish nohow, least of all raw—huh?"

He struggled into a sitting position.

"Hey," he said quickly, and stared hard at a huddled figure that lay just beyond him. "Who—who's that?"

"Him? Oh, that's th' guard," Marshall answered.

"Oh, yeah? What's he doin' here—soldierin' on th' job?"

"On'y in a way, Dee."

"Wa-al, whatever that way is, he's sleepin'," Dee retorted. He turned his head suddenly and gave Marshall a sidelong glance. "Who sang 'im th' lullaby—you?"

"It wasn't th' sandman."

"H'm. Then he's havin' nightmares 'stead o' sweet dreams. What happened, an' what'd yuh yank th' rope f'r? This here sleepin' beauty show up again?"

"Yep. Soon's I heard 'im comin' I jerked th' line. It was th' on'y way I could tip yuh off that comp'ny was comin'," Marshall replied.

The puncher snorted.

"Some comp'ny! A danged busybody, who got what was comin' to 'im. Mebbe that'll learn 'im not t' barge in on folks again. Say, Marshall!"

"Yeah—what?"

"Take off that feller's boots, will yuh? He don't know it, but we're gonna swap clothes, him an' me, right here an' now! Doggone—this is better'n I expected!"

Marshall stepped around him and bent over the motionless guard. He jerked off one boot, and followed with its mate. When he looked up again, Dee had whipped off his jacket and shirt, and was peeling off his undershirt. It was a minute's work to remove the guard's clothes, another minute's work for Dee to don them. He climbed to his feet presently.

"Say—this is awright, y'know? This feller's somethin' of a dude. Lookit them fancy pants," he said. He thrust his hands into the pockets. "Huh! Mighta knowed it, doggone it! Fancy pants an' nuthin' in his pockets!"

Marshall laughed lightly.

"S'ppose we get goin' again, Dee? We've wasted a heap o' time a'ready."

"Right with yuh, Marshall. Hey—didn't this feller tote a gun o' some kind? I oughta have one, y'know. Can't use mine 'cause it's soaked."

"Yeah, come t' think of it; Dee, he had a rifle," Marshall replied. He turned and looked along the grassy bank. "It's layin' along there somewheres."

"That so? Say—don't tell me th' skunk was fixin' t' drill me while I was nearly drownin' out there!"

"Dunno f'r sure, Dee, just what he was plannin' t' do. All I could see was that he had 'is gun raised. That's when I stepped in."

"Why, th' dirty dog! I oughta kick 'is teeth in!"

Marshall laughed again.

"S'ppose yuh hustle out there instead, Dee, an' get 'is rifle? Oh, yeah—bring that rope back here, too, will yuh?"

The puncher turned and trudged off. He returned shortly, rifle in hand, the rope trailing along behind him.

"Gonna tie 'im up?" he asked, nodding toward the man whose clothes he had taken.

"Yeah."

"Want me t' do it?"

"D'yuh mind?"

Dee snorted loudly in reply. Quickly he put down the rifle. He bent over the man, gave him a mighty shove and rolled him over on his face, straddled him and proceeded to tie him up. Marshall watched quietly, amusedly. Dee grunted with satisfaction each time he jerked a knot tight. Finally, finished, he tested his handiwork, straightened up and stepped back.

"There," he said. "That'll hold 'im, b'lieve me. He'll never bust 'is way outta that 'less someb'dy blasts 'im out."

The tail of the man's shirt—Dee protested mildly before he surrendered it—was jammed into the guard's mouth to prevent an outcry from him when he regained consciousness. Then, with Marshall again in the lead, they stepped out from their place of concealment and made their way up toward the trees. They avoided striking directly for the entrance—a precaution against running into a possible relief guard coming on duty. Directly behind the trees there was thick brush which formed a solid wall, shutting out the ranch from prying eyes. Quietly, although sometimes the needle-pointed briars tore at them painfully, they pushed their way forward through the brush, halting finally to peer out, their eyes ranging over the place.

There were two tall, dark, hulking barns straight ahead, and two small shacks, low, squat and equally darkened, just beyond the barns. The bunkhouse, a long, low structure, stood on the left, just about midway between the entrance to the ranch and the hulking barns; the ranchhouse was directly opposite the bunkhouse. There were lights visible in both buildings.

"Looks like nob'dy turned in," Dee muttered. "What d'we do now, Marshall?"

Marshall had been studying the ranchhouse.

"Like's not," he answered shortly, nodding toward the ranchhouse, "June's in there somewheres. I'm gonna sneak outta here an' kinda mosey for'ard a bit an' have a look around while you—"

"While I what?"

"You stay put here."

"Oh, yeah?"

"Yeah. You got th' rifle. You stay here an' keep me covered 'case I run into somethin' an' hafta backtrack. Get th' idea?"

"Yeah, but I don't like it. Two of us t'gether'd be a heap better'n just one of us if yuh run inter trouble."

"We're wastin' valu'ble time again, Dee, arguin' here. S'ppose we do like I s'ggested?"

"Wa-al, awright," Dee mumbled. "I shoulda knowed somethin' like this'd happen."

"Quit beefin'. Th' chances are they'll have guards posted aroun' th' ranchhouse an' I'll hafta backtrack in a hurry."

"Then mind that yuh do. You get back here soon's yuh see what's doin' 'round there an' lemme know."

"I will, Dee, soon's I can. On'y keep yore shirt on an' don't go gettin' impatient if I don't come back right off. It'll be comfortin' t' know that if anythin' should happen, you'll be here with that Winchester primed t' speak its piece."

CHAPTER 17

THE ROPE flashed upward with the darting speed and deadly accuracy of a striking snake. The noose seemed to widen as it hovered over the chimney; then it settled gently around it and suddenly snapped taut. Marshall came up swiftly, actually "walking" up the side of the building, for he used the rope simply as a hoist as his booted feet trod up the shingled side of the ranchhouse. He paused momentarily whenever he came abreast of a lighted window, and peered inside quickly; when he failed to see June, he frowned and climbed higher. Already in his mind he knew exactly what he would do when he reached the roof, provided, of course, that he failed to spot June before that. He would shift the rope and lower it down the opposite side of the house and have a look into the windows there. He looked up. He was nearing the roof. He reached for it with one hand and pulled himself in close, swung one leg over it and rolled onto it. Quickly he scrambled to his feet.

He drew up the dangling rope, slung it over his shoulder and started toward the chimney, halted abruptly and stared hard. There was something beside the chimney, far down, almost at its very base. He studied it for a moment, wondering what it was. He shrugged his shoulders finally and plodded on again, came up to the chimney, stopped and looked down. His eyes widened. A human figure was huddling there against the chimney, a hatless, coated figure with its face buried in its upturned collar. He dropped the rope, leaped back and whipped out a big Colt.

"Awright!" he snapped. "Get up outta there—an' keep yore hands high!"

There was no response. Marshall was motionless for a moment; then he edged his way forward again, his gun levelled and ready. He nudged the huddled form and quickly stepped back.

"P-st!" he hissed.

The tousled head of a woman jerked up. Marshall dropped to one knee beside her.

"June!"

Her heavy-lidded, sleep-laden eyes stared at him, widened. . . .

"Marshall!" she threw herself into his arms and clung to him, sobbing against his chest. "I knew you'd come for me—I knew it, I knew it!"

He held her close for a moment, patting her shoulder.

"Now, now, yuh don't wanna cry. Ain't no one gonna hurt yuh now. Yuh know I wouldn't let 'em."

She raised her head a bit.

"Handkerchief," he heard her say.

He dug inside his coat and finally drew out a bandana.

"Here y'are, June."

She sat up, took the bandana and dabbed at her eyes and nose.

"Blow it," he said authoritatively.

She obeyed—and finally looked up at him.

"Better hol' on to it," he said. "I got 'nother one on me somewheres. Now then, yuh awright? Think yuh're able t' get goin'?"

"Oh, yes," she said quickly.

"Good girl."

He straightened up, lifted her to her feet, caught up the rope again and led her to the edge of the roof.

"Scared?" he asked, nodding earthward.

"No, not any more."

"Good f'r you. I'm gonna let you go down first. I'll tie this aroun' yuh good an' tight. Th' minute yore feet touch th' ground, yank it off an' beat it away fr'm here. There're s'me trees close by—head f'r 'em an' wait there f'r me. If somethin' happens—if I can't make it right off—get goin' again, fast's yuh can, understan'? Dee Miles is waitin' in th' brush t' th' left of th' entrance. Yuh gotta reach him, June—he'll see to it that yuh get away safe."

She stood close to him, looking up at him.

"But you—you'll come down right away, won't you?" she asked.

"Shore will," he replied. He looped the rope around her waist and jerked the knot tight. "Ready?"

"Ready," she said simply.

"I'm gonna set yuh down on th' edge o' th' roof with yore legs danglin' over," he explained in a low tone. "When I say 'awright,' turn over on yore tummy. Understan'?"

"Yes."

He bent, lifted her in his arms, and set her down gently on the very edge of the roof.

"Don't look down," he said quickly, "if yuh think it'll scare yuh."

"It won't," she answered over her shoulder.

"Just as yuh say. Awright now."

Unhesitatingly June twisted around until she was flat on her stomach. Her legs dangled uncertainly in space. The rope jerked sharply upward, brushing her face. She raised her hands, caught hold of it, tightened her grip; then she was swung off the roof. Slowly she went down, passing directly between two lighted windows. She caught her breath and dared not look to either side. Then she was passing still another lighted window, and finally her feet were on the ground again.

Quickly, without so much as an over-the-shoulder glance about her, she tore open the slip knot, cast off the rope, wheeled and darted away. The trees which Marshall had spoken of were but a dozen feet beyond the house. She headed for them, stumbled over a half buried rock but managed to keep her feet,

112

swerved sharply and flung herself behind a sturdy trunk and crouched down.

Suddenly there was a shout from somewhere within the house. She heard a pane of glass shatter, got to her feet and looked up. Her heart pounded up into her throat. A shadowy figure was dangling from a rope midway between the two lighted windows. And a man was astride the sill of one of the windows, leaning out, trying to catch hold of one of Marshall's legs. Marshall jerked himself away, just managing to evade the man's outstretched hand. Then June saw still another man appear—he had evidently rushed out of the house. As she watched with bated breath, she saw him skid to a halt directly beneath Marshall, saw him grab at the rope and jerk it viciously. Marshall suddenly came plunging down. A scream broke from June's lips. She wheeled and fled.

Somehow she managed to reach the brush to the left of the entrance—Marshall's instructions were still ringing in her ears. She tripped and fell to her knees. Someone bent over her, lifted her to her feet and half dragged, half carried her into the brush.

"Yuh awright?" she heard a voice ask. It was Dee Miles.

"Y-yes," she panted.

"What happened back there? Did yuh see Marshall? Where is he?" the puncher asked quickly.

"They've caught him," she gasped.

"Oh, yeah? Look, June—you c'n ride, can'tcha? Yuh game t' go f'r help?" he went on.

"Of course."

"It's our on'y chance t' save Marshall, if them polecats 've caught 'im," he went on. "Our horses are on th' other side o' that creek or whatever th' danged thing is, 'bout a hundred feet up along th' bank fr'm th' bridge. Anyway, don't monkey aroun' with Marshall's horse—that black o' his is plain hell on hoofs. Take mine. He ain't exactly a ladies' horse; still, once yuh're on 'im, he won't cut up none."

"Go on, Dee," she urged impatiently.

"Wa-al, once yuh get goin' head f'r th' Circle D," Miles continued. "When yuh get there, rouse th' boys an' tell 'em what's happenin'. Meanwhile I'll try t' keep things goin' 'round here 'til they show up. Think yuh c'n make it?"

"I'll make it, all right," she answered grimly.

" 'Course yuh will," he said heartily. "C'mon—I'll show yuh where t' go. Stick close t' me, June, an' keep yore head down an' yore hands over yore face. This brush is ornery. Th' briars are like claws—give 'em half a chance t' reach yuh an' they'll cut yore face t' ribbons. Let's go."

Marshall landed on top of the man. They went down in a heap with legs threshing and kicking and arms swinging. Marshall rolled away and staggered to his feet—his opponent scrambled up, too. There was a knife in his hand; its long blade gleamed with a steely brightness. He crouched, gathering himself together, and took a single cat-like step forward, a step that was a warning in itself. Marshall, watching him carefully, was prepared for what was to follow. His right hand had dropped—now it hung crab-like an inch above the jutting butt of his gun. As the man leaped at him, Marshall fired from the hip. The man stumbled, halted awkwardly, falteringly, in his tracks and tottered a bit. He dropped his knife; stiffened, seemed to rise up on his toes, then suddenly pitched forward on his face. Marshall side-stepped nimbly.

A gun roared from a point overhead, and a bullet spat and whined past his head. He ducked instinctively and twisted away from the spot, whirled and fired upward. A gun fell harmlessly at his feet. The man who had mounted the window sill on the upper floor and who had sought so desperately to seize him by the leg as he came down the rope tumbled from his perch. He struck the ground with a dull thud, toppled over and finally slumped down in a sprawled heap.

There were shouts now from various points about the place. The bunkhouse door was flung open and men poured out. Marshall hesitated for a moment, looking quickly, anxiously toward the trees beyond the house. There was no sign there of June. He turned again, this time toward the entrance to the ranch. There was no one there. He breathed easier. Evidently June had followed his instructions implicitly—she had simply scampered away as he had told her to when he had failed to join her as agreed. The shooting, he decided, had probably hastened her flight. Doubtless, too, she had managed to find Dee Miles, and the puncher in turn had promptly whisked her away to safety.

Now, with June out of harm's reach, half of Marshall's mission was accomplished; the second half, and certainly it was by far the more difficult of the two, still awaited his attention. Freedom for June was not sufficient. There would never be any great degree of permanency attached to such freedom as long as Jess Barnes and his men were left intact and as long as they were permitted to hole up on the Bar JH. They would have to be routed out, broken up, scattered; even then, as individuals, they would always constitute a threat. Actually, and for the sake of permanent safety for June, they would have to be disposed of completely. Just how that minor miracle would be brought about, Marshall refused to venture an opinion. Approaching footsteps now caused him to move quickly for his own safety.

He holstered his gun, wheeled and bolted away, racing around the rear of the house. He swung wide of it, his eye on the back door as he sprinted past. If the door opened and further opposition appeared, he would be prepared to deal with it. Then, too, whoever burst out of the house with a view toward halting him would present an easily hit target outlined against the lighted house. On the other hand, if he kept within the shadows, he would be little more than a fleeting, flitting shadow himself, blending with the night light. But the door did not open. In another moment he was safely past the house.

He headed for the two hulking barns, plunged into the dark passageway between them and went crashing into a sturdily built chest that refused to be dislodged. He sprawled over it awkwardly.

"Damnation," he mumbled through gritted teeth. He rubbed his right knee and shin bone tenderly, wincing when he touched a particularly sore spot. "Nob'dy but a mangy, ornery, locoed cuss'd leave anythin' like that standin' aroun' f'r a feller t' fall over. I'd shore like t' get m' hands on th' skunk that left it there. He'd never leave 'nything else standin' aroun', not even 'imself, when I got finished with 'im, b'lieve me."

He hitched up his pants angrily, gave his hat a vicious tug and plodded off. Presently he halted a second time and rubbed his leg again, then suddenly straightened up and looked back over his shoulder. He was strangely curious about the chest. He had seen similar ones before, many of them, as a matter of fact; usually explosives were stored in them. He trudged back, falteringly, favoring the injured leg, halted in front of the chest and tried the lid. It was unlocked and yielded at once to his touch. He raised it, bent down and thrust his hand inside its dark depths. On the very bottom of the chest his groping fingers found something. He touched the thing again, carefully.

"Boy!" he said aloud, jubilantly. "Dynamite!"

He threw the lid back now, bent down again and scooped up the stick of dynamite. He probed the chest from corner to corner, and when he straightened up again there were six sticks in his hand.

"I'll shore raise plenty o' hell with this stuff!" he muttered.

He tore open his jacket and shoved the sticks into his shirt. Loud shouts were now audible from the direction of the house —evidently the bodies of the two men had been found. It was quite likely too that June's escape had been discovered. He started off again, slackening his pace to a hobble for his leg ached badly.

He had trudged about half a mile when he heard the lowing of cattle somewhere close by. He halted and looked about, trying to locate the herd. A grove of trees loomed up just ahead of him; the lowing grew louder as he neared them. He found himself going downhill, noticed too that the air was increasingly cooler the further down he went. He decided that the atmospheric change was due to the nearness of a body of water, doubtless the river itself. A steer brushed past him with startling suddenness, and Marshall twisted away hastily. Other steers lumbered by. Marshall was puzzled. What were steers doing in such a place? Why weren't they in the corral?

He tripped over a rock, stumbled against a steer, and the animal shied away in fright. Its mates swerved away from Marshall, too, even increased their ungainly stride.

Suddenly he was pitched into complete darkness. He looked up quickly, skyward, but he could see nothing. He stumbled again, jerked himself away from what was probably a half buried rock and promptly bumped into a wall. He backed away from it, bent down and groped for something along the ground. He picked up a small stone and tossed it upward, heard it strike something overhead, a ceiling evidently, then fall to earth a foot or two beyond him. Immediately he decided that he was in a tunnel, perhaps a spacious cave. Presently he noticed that his eyes were growing accustomed to the darkness. He was able to make out the individual forms of lumbering, plodding cattle. There were many of them; they formed a long, almost endless double line.

He jerked to an awkward halt when he heard the rumble of rifle fire somewhere in the distance beyond him. He happened to glance at the steers and noticed with surprise that they had halted, too. He looked up quickly when he heard approaching hoofs beats, and backed quickly against the wall, his hands curled around the butts of his guns. The clatter of iron hoofs increased. A shadowy, indistinguishable horseman trotted past him, then another. Obviously the outburst of gunfire had aroused their curiosity, too. They disappeared in the darkness.

He heard gunfire again, more thunderous than before; then another blast, evidently an answering volley. Shouts resounded from the direction of the entrance to the tunnel, then the clatter of hoof beats. It sounded like a whole party of horsemen rather than just the two men who had ridden past him.

For a brief moment he was motionless, thoughtfully still. Then he whirled suddenly and darted away, recklessly indifferent to the darkness and to the hazards of the trail ahead. Finally he spied a light ahead of him—the light of a clearing sky. He was then just about abreast of the idling leaders of the waiting column of steers and about a hundred feet from the exit of the tunnel. He was panting hard, but he plunged on, sprinting as never before, completely forgetting that only a short time before he had been limping. He burst out of the tunnel and into the open. He could hear the plunging thunder of a waterfall somewhere beyond him. There were trees and boulders on both sides of him; in that moment he noticed too that the terrain was rough, rocky and mountainous. He wheeled, and fumbled inside his shirt for a stick of dynamite. The idling cattle were now distant and shadowy figures in the gloom of the darkened tunnel.

He gripped the stick in his right hand, drew back his arm and hurled the explosive into the tunnel. There was a terrific explosion—one that rocked the very ground—a blinding flash and a thunderous crash. He turned his head quickly, threw his arms over his face and head. Smoke and dust swirled around him. After a minute he peered out. The smoke was lifting gently, while the dust, now knee-high, was beginning to settle. There was, he quickly noted, panic inside the tunnel. The steers, terror-stricken, were turning this way and that, trampling and butting their mates, biting and kicking in a frantic effort to get away. A second stick of dynamite produced even greater turmoil. The steers finally broke and went thundering back through the tunnel. Marshall dashed after them.

There was more gunfire now—not thunderous volleys as before, but the sharp, distinct crashing of individual rifles. Now, too, the pounding of headlong hoofs seemed to lessen—evidently the frenzied rush of the fear-maddened cattle had been checked. Marshall raced on, slackening his pace when he heard the wheezing panting of cattle just ahead of him. He whipped out a big Colt and fired twice into the wall opposite him. The steers lurched forward again. Marshall caught a glimpse of shadowy horsemen in the entrance, in the very path of the surging cattle. There were gun flashes from the entrance and cries of pain from the steers, but there was no halting them now. They swept out of the tunnel like a swift-running tide, carrying everything before them.

CHAPTER 18

IT WAS almost dawn now.

Gun leveled and ready, Marshall emerged from the darkness of the tunnel and halted just inside the entrance. Half a dozen steers lay on the ground, rigidly stiff in death. Pools of blood had formed beneath their heads and bodies. A dozen feet away lay a horse; his sprawled rider lay just beyond him, his booted foot caught in his horse's reins. A bit farther up the incline were the bodies of two more men. One of them lay on his back, his arms outflung, his face a battered, bloodied mass. His companion's body, as limp as a bag of meal, lay huddled just beyond him.

There was a faint whinny just outside the tunnel. Marshall edged forward and peered out cautiously. A horse lay to the left of the entrance. His right foreleg was doubled up under his body awkwardly, evidently broken. He raised his head again and whinnied a second time, subsided for a moment, then suddenly threshed about wildly, struggling to get up. He sank down again presently, his sides heaving furiously, whimpered and finally lay still.

There was no firing now; however, the echo of crashing guns seemed to linger in the air. There was a strong, pungent smell of burnt gunpowder in the air, too. Marshall made his way up the incline, circling the bodies of the dead men warily, giving each an over-the-shoulder glance as he trudged past, quickened his pace when he reached level ground again, dashed forward through the trees and halted finally on the very fringe of the wooded section. There was no sound, no sign of anyone. He went on again, retracing his former route, trudged into the passageway between the towering barns and halted in his tracks when a man, rifle in hand, backed around the corner of one of the barns. His Colt flashed upward, and the man wheeled. It was Dee Miles. Marshall lowered his gun. Dee, grinning happily, rushed up to him.

"Marshall!" he exclaimed delightedly. "Yuh son-of-a-gun! Doggone it, man—I never expected t' see you alive again! I had it figgered out that Barnes an' th' others had finished you off. Tell me—whatcha been doin' with y'self all this while? Where've yuh been—huh?"

Marshall laughed softly.

"One thing at a time, Dee," he responded. "I've been around—seein' things an' doin' things. How 'bout you? How'd you manage t' get in here? An' by th' way, what was all that shootin' I heard b'fore?"

The puncher gave him a sly, sidelong glance.

"Don'tcha wanna know 'bout June Halliday first?" he asked.

"June?" Marshall echoed. "'Course I do. She's safe, ain't she?"

"She shore is."

"Awright then. Get me up t' date on th' other doin's 'round here," Marshall commanded.

"I'm comin' to 'em. First off, June went back to th' Circle D f'r help. Everybody come an' come pronto. The boys are scattered all aroun' here, so watch yore step, Marshall, an' don't go tramplin' on any o' them."

"Go on, Dee—go on. We don't wanna stan' 'round here all day, y'know, gabbin' like a couple o' ol' women."

"Wa-al," Dee began again, "soon's th' boys showed up, we

slipped in an' s'rrounded th' bunkhouse an' th' ranchhouse both. Nob'dy got wise t' us bein' here till some o' th' hellions who'd been out chasin' you come wanderin' back an' ran into some o' our boys. We went t' work on 'em pronto an' poured hot lead into 'em 'till they just broke an' started t' run f'r it. We musta got most of 'em. Yuh wanna see th' way they're sprawled out in front o' th' bunkhouse—thicker'n flies on a mule. Anyway, someb'dy said that on'y one o' them got away. Couple o' th' boys went after 'im, but they lost 'im somewheres."

"Uh-huh. Anythin' else?"

"Nope—that's 'bout all there is t' tell, Marshall. Couple o' them are still around, holed up in th' ranchhouse. How many there are, I dunno."

"Seen anythin' o' Barnes?"

"Nope."

"How 'bout Pecos?"

"That polecat? Ain't seen anythin' o' him either."

"Then th' chances are they're th' ones holed up."

"Yeah, I s'ppose so. What d'yuh think we oughta do? 'Course we could smoke 'em out—that'd drive 'em out into th' open— on'y that'd mean burnin' down th' house."

Marshall shook his head.

"That's out," he said with finality. "There must be another way o' doin' it."

Dee shrugged his shoulder.

"Awright—you tell me what it is."

Marshall busied himself reloading his gun, fanned it expertly and returned it to his holster.

"So what?" Dee asked.

"I'm gonna slip into th' house," Marshall announced simply. "Fr'm th' rear."

The puncher frowned.

"I don't think much o' that idea."

Marshall disregarded Dee's comment.

"Once I'm inside," he went on calmly, "I oughta be able t' rout 'em out."

"Yeah—if yuh get inside," Dee said dryly.

"I'll get in awright," Marshall said confidently. "You get word t' th' boys t' start blastin' away at th' house so's to attract Barnes' attention—his an' whoever else is in there with

120

him. That'll make it easy f'r me t' bust in on 'em. Get th' idea now?"

The puncher's comment took the form of a grunt.

"How 'bout me goin' along with yuh?" he asked.

"Nope. This is a one-man job. If we both went, one of us'd get in th' other's way. This is gonna be quick—an' I either do what I'm settin' out t' do—or I don't."

The puncher grinned at him.

"G'wan, get goin'. I'll go pass th' word along t' th' boys."

Marshall nodded and turned away.

"Marshall!"

He halted and looked back over his shoulder.

"Watch y'self—understan'?"

Marshall grinned, turned and strode briskly away. He broke into a run presently and headed due north. Far ahead of him the trees loomed up. He swerved suddenly, just as a rifle cracked, and swung eastward. There were some thick clumps of brush along the way, and he darted behind them, bending as low as he could without slackening his pace. Then there was a sudden blast of rifle fire, which swelled with each passing second.

He swung away again, swerving sharply toward the rear of the house. The booming of the guns continued. He was grateful for the trees behind the house, for they provided the very protection he needed now. He reached the first tree safely and leaped on to the next, pausing behind each for a quick look at the house; then, reasonably certain that he still hadn't been detected, dashed on again, getting closer to his objective all the time. There was a patch of open ground between the trees and the house, and he sprinted across the intervening space, and came panting up to the back door.

He tried the knob. It turned easily, and the door opened. In a flash he was over the threshold. He closed the door behind him quietly, and glanced around the room. It was a neatly arranged kitchen; however, there were dirty dishes on the table, and a soiled knife lay directly beneath it. He heard heavy footsteps overhead, then the roar of a rifle; the explosion rocked the house. There was a stairway at the far end of the room. He jerked out his guns, tiptoed across the room and halted when he reached the stairway. He was motionless for a moment, listening intently, then finally started up the stairs, halting on each step and cursing under his breath because the stairway creaked beneath him. If only the Circle D men would continue shooting! Then, as though in immediate response to his wish, there was a sudden and terrific blast of gunfire outside. Somewhere in the house a pane of glass shattered and crashed. Taking full advantage of the din, he bounded up the stairs to the upper floor.

He looked about him quickly. There was a small, curtained window at the far end of the floor, and two rooms, one on each side of the stairway. The doors of the rooms were closed. He heard a rifle crack inside the room on his left, and turned toward it at once, his guns leveled and ready. He tiptoed across the narrow hallway floor, and whirled like a flash when he heard the opposite door open. He threw himself sideways, his gun flaming from his hip. He had caught a glimpse of a tall figure in the open doorway; the man had reached for his gun, too, and had even managed to jerk it clear of his holster before Marshall fired. The man tottered, sagged against the door jamb; then slowly and painfully he straightened up and raised his gun. Marshall's Colt thundered a second time. The heavy slug blasted the man backwards. The door swung shut behind him. Marshall backed away.

There was a sudden creaking, and the other door opened a bit. After a cautious pause, it was opened wider, and a man peered out. It was Pecos! He caught sight of Marshall framed against the opposite wall, facing him, and hastily withdrew his head and slammed the door shut.

"Reckon that's that," Marshall muttered to himself. "It ain't a s'rprise any more. Now they know they've got comp'ny."

He had already decided upon his course of action, now that his presence had been discovered. Quickly he stepped across the hallway and flattened out against the wall. He crept closer to the door and listened there for a moment, but he could hear nothing from within the room. Even the purposeful shooting outside had ceased. Evidently Dee was satisfied that Marshall had managed to reach and enter the house.

He straightened up, shifting his guns in his hands. The twin Colts thundered with startling suddenness. A heavy slug tore the knob away from the door. It struck the floor, bounced against the door, caromed off and rolled down the stairs. The second bullet smashed the flimsy lock; a third drove it completely through the door. Marshall heard it fall to the floor inside the room. He fired twice more, and the upper and lower hinges of the door were smashed to bits. There was a ripping, tearing sound as the door tore loose from the broken hinges. Quickly again Marshall stepped forward, gave the door a lusty kick and promptly whirled away. The door fell in with a crash.

Marshall retreated, cramming fresh cartridges into his guns. He was ready again in another moment.

A stocky man—it was Pecos again—came plunging out, his gun leveled. His first shot tore into the opposite wall. Too late he realized that he had been outwitted, and that his target had moved. He wheeled instantly. A single Colt thundered mightily before Pecos, who had just sighted his missing target, could fire. Pecos went down on his hands and knees. He shook his head as though he were clearing it and looked up. Swallowing hard, he tightened his grip on his gun butt, and had raised his gun when the Colt roared again. A shudder ran through the swarthy man's body. His gun slid out of his hand, and he pitched forward on his face. His left leg twitched once; then he lay still.

Marshall turned toward the open doorway. Barnes would have to emerge now. A full minute passed, but there was no sign of him, no sound from within the room.

"Barnes!" Marshall called.

There was no reply.

"Barnes!" Marshall called again, louder.

Still there was no response.

"Awright, Barnes—if that's th' way yuh want it, that's just th' way it's gonna be. I'm comin' in after yuh!"

Marshall had edged closer to the open doorway. He halted within inches of it and waited again, but only for a moment; then he suddenly leaped over the threshold and into the room. There was a roar of gunfire, the thunder of point-blank shooting. It was over in less than a minute. There was a heavy, oppressive silence; then someone sighed. A table was shoved aside; there was a single footstep, a faltering step, a pause; then a body crashed heavily to the floor.

Gun smoke curled lazily ceilingward from the muzzles of the big Colts. Marshall, crouching, watched the sprawled, face downward figure on the floor. After a minute, apparently satisfied that his work was done, Marshall straightened up.

Slowly he holstered his guns. He looked down at the motionless body of Jess Barnes.

"Wa'al, Barnes," he said. "Reckon this is th' end o' th' trail f'r you. Mebbe there'll be s'me peace in Paradise an' 'round here, too."

He turned slowly and trudged to the door.

Marshall dismounted in front of the house, spied Dee Miles on the porch and trudged up the steps to join him.

"Looks like th' boys've been right busy 'round here," Marshall remarked. "Place looks pretty much t' rights a'ready."

"Oh, shore," Dee replied. "I sent f'r that undertaker feller fr'm Paradise t' come out here f'r Barnes an' th' others. He shore had a wagonload when he left here. Reckon Boot Hill's plumb full up now. Folks'll simply halfta stay alive now, leastways till someb'dy sets up a new cemetery b'fore they c'n die an' hope t' be planted away proper."

"How 'bout inside th' house? Did yuh have that door fixed like I told yuh to?"

"I did more'n that, Marshall. Hank Denning's right handy with tools, y'know. I told 'im t' go through th' hull house an' see what needed fixin' an t' hop to it. He did a swell job, awright—wait'll yuh see it. June won't have a thing t' c'mplain about or do. Everything's in order f'r 'er. Tell me—how were things at th' Circle D? Awright?"

"Yes an' no."

"Huh? What's that s'pposed t' mean?"

"Stella's dead," Marshall said quietly.

Dee stared hard at him.

"Stella's what?" he demanded.

"You heard what I said," Marshall retorted.

"If yuh said that Stella Davis is dead, then I heard yuh awright. But, ding bust it, Marshall—what'n hell happened to 'er?"

"Wa'al," Marshall began, "just keep yore shirt on an' I'll tell yuh. It seems that just after th' boys lit outta there f'r here, June went to th' barn t' saddle up that mare o' hers. She wasn't gonna stay put there while we were up here fightin' for her. She d'cided she wanted t' take a hand in th' pr'ceedings too."

"Good f'r her."

124

"Yeah, she's got plenty o' nerve. Anyway, Stella follered her into th' barn an' jumped on 'er."

"No!"

"Yes, an' with a knife, too," Marshall went on, grimly. "They wrestled aroun' some, with Stella screamin' like a wild woman, callin' 'er names, accusin' 'er of this an' that, an' strugglin' t' get her knife hand free, while June was hangin' on to it f'r all she was worth. All of a sudden one o' them slipped an' both o' them went down, one on top o' the other. June got up, awright, soon's she could, but Stella didn't—she couldn't. Th' knife was plunged into 'er clear up to th' hilt."

"I'll be damned!"

"June managed somehow t' get Stella up to th' house, got her into bed, too, an' did what she could for 'er. She wanted to ride up here f'r help, but Stella begged her not to leave her. Reckon she musta knowed she was done f'r an' that it was on'y a matter o' time. She was dyin' when I got there. She talked some b'fore she cashed in."

"Oh, yeah? She say anythin' worth r'peatin'?"

"Oh, on'y that she was th' one who helped Pecos escape. Seems she had some fool idea 'bout bein' in love with me an' that June was cuttin' 'er out—or some such damn foolishness. She figgered that if she helped Pecos get away he'd be more'n willin' t' kidnap June an' get her outta th' way. How d'yuh like that, Dee?"

"That's th' damnedest thing I ever heard; still, it don't s'rprise me none, Marshall. Women are queer folks sometimes, d'yuh know that? They c'n get th' dangedest ideas an' do th' dangedest things. What'd yuh do with Stella?"

"On'y thing I could do. I buried 'er right alongside of 'er husband. Reckon fr'm now on he won't hafta do much worryin' about 'er. He'll allus know where she's at, who she's with an' what she's doin'. That'll be a heap more'n he ever knew about 'er b'fore, I'll bet."

It was a bright, full, silvery moon that peered down over the distant mountain top. The sky was filled with gay, twinkling stars sparkling in a canopy of blue.

June leaned over the railing of the bridge and stared down at the water in the moat. Marshall stood beside her—so close

125

that their elbows touched—his broad back against the rail, the heel of his right boot hooked over the lower rung of the rail. There was a strong, swirling current in the moat, silver-crested in the bright moonlight; the water swept inland from the river overpoweringly. She watched it with a curious and almost fierce intentness, watched the miniature rollers until they darted under the bridge and disappeared beyond it.

"Then you're still determined to go on to California?" she asked finally without looking up.

"Oh, shore," Marshall replied.

"But why, Marshall? California's so far away, so completely new and strange, so—"

"Mebbe that's why I'm so anxious t' go there," he interrupted. "I know it don't make sense t' you, June; mebbe it even seems loco t' you f'r anyone t' go chasin' after somethin' they can't even explain. But there's somethin' about it, even about th' thought of it, that stirs me, makes m' blood race an' m' heart beat faster. I s'ppose yuh might call it adventure—but whatever it is, th' thought of it grips me an'—wa-al, that's why I'm goin'."

She lapsed into silence then. They could hear the wash of the swift current as it broke over the banks of the moat.

"Of course you'll be coming back again soon, at least some day, won't you?" she asked presently.

"*Quien sabe?*"

"But isn't there something—or someone—you'll miss and will want to return to?" she asked.

"Yeah, I s'ppose so."

"Would it be—a girl?"

He straightened up, turned her around gently, and looked down into her earnest young face.

"June," he began, "lemme tell yuh somethin'. Mebbe it'll hurt some, but that'll on'y be in th' b'ginnin'. Afterwards yuh'll be glad. Awright?"

She nodded mutely.

"June," he went on, "th' girl who gives up everythin' f'r me can't get anythin' out of it but th' worst. I know what I'm talkin' about. 'Course it don't mean that I'm that diff'rent fr'm other men that I don't want a wife an' a home an' mebbe a flock o' kids. I do—heck, yes—but I ain't got t' give what a real married life, a happy one, d'mands of a man. Y'know, June, ever since I c'n r'member, I've allus been restless an' impatient, allus wantin' t' be up an' doin' an' goin' places, never able t' stay put anywhere f'r long. Somehow, no matter which way I turn, my eyes are allus lookin' to'ard th' horizon, tryin' t' see what lays b'hind an' b'yond it."

"But, Marshall," she said doggedly, "if the right girl—"
He shook his head.

"No, June, I ain't th' right kind of a man f'r any girl. What kind of a life would a girl have with me—no home, nuthin' much of anythin', allus movin' on an' on, allus chasin' after somethin' I can't even describe."

"But there's bound to come a day—"

"When I'll be fed up with roamin' an' wish I had somethin' like other men? 'Course there will—an' I'll be th' one t' blame f'r not havin' it. But on th' other hand, it'll be a heap easier t' take if I'm th' on'y one t' suffer an' not some girl who thought she could change me an' broke 'er heart tryin'. No, June, it's no go. It won't work."

Her head came down now, against his chest.

"You f'rget all about me, June," he continued. "Yuh're all set now—yuh got th' ranch back an' nob'dy'll ever take it away fr'm yuh again, not with Dee Miles an' th' rest o' th' boys workin' f'r yuh. Then, too, right now yuh got more cattle'n Jim Halliday ever had, what with th' Circle D herd thrown in, since there's nob'dy aroun' t' come claim 'em."

He patted her arm gently.

"One o' these fine days—y'know, June, th' range is fillin' up with lots o' decent folks fr'm th' East—some smart young feller, someb'dy like you, 'll come ridin' right over this here bridge an' right smack into yore heart. He'll be everything that I wanted t' be an' ain't—you'll see. Then yuh'll be glad yuh didn't throw y'self away on th' likes o' me, b'lieve me."

He turned his head and looked toward the ranch.

"Say, it must be gettin' late. Th' light in th' bunkhouse is out. Go on, June—turn aroun' an' trot up t' bed. You must be plumb tuckered out by now."

She raised her head.

"I'll—I'll see you in the morning?"

"No. I aim t' be gone b'fore sunup."

She suddenly threw her arms around his neck and clung to

him tightly. His arms came up, too, holding her close. Her lips sought his, found them and clung to them. Time stood still for that one glorious, parting kiss. Then she turned slowly, trudged up the gravel incline and disappeared among the shadow-shrouded trees.